BLOOD-SPILLER'S QUARRY
A NOVEL OF THE
STONE LAW

Airship 27 Productions

Blood-Spiller's Quarry
a novel of the Stone Law

© 2023 Michael Panush

Published by Airship 27 Productions
www.airship27.com
www.airship27hangar.com

Interior and cover illustrations © 2023 Earl Geier
Cover coloring by Rob Davis

Editor: Ron Fortier
Associate Editor: Gordon Dymowski
Marketing and Promotions Manager: Michael Vance
Production Designer: Rob Davis

ISBN: 978-1-953589-53-8

Printed in the United States of America

10 9 8 7 6 5 4 3 2 1

BLOOD-SPILLER'S QUARRY
A NOVEL OF THE
STONE LAW

BY MICHAEL PANUSH

CHAPTER ONE
A SEED IS PLANTED IN A DEAD MAN'S MOUTH

The monkey lay dead and half-decaying in the dirt, the flies and ants just emerging from the tall grass below the taller trees. They weren't the only ones who wanted the monkey. Two Thin Ones from the Heap squatted on both sides of the dead creature, full of hatred, with death in their fingers. Squint Eye, a good hunter until a kick from an aurochs' hoof had left the right half of his face swollen and broken, and Gaunt—an ash-haired Thin Nose who looked like he had never gotten enough to eat.

They both wanted that monkey—the fur and the flesh. They'd fight each other to get it, with the easy way that Thin Noses turned to violence.

And I had to stop them.

"I saw it first!" Squint Eye had a slight slur in his words. He had a stone axe at his belt, and shifted his deer skin vest to get at it. His words echoed up the pathway, leading out of the forest and to the base of the Heap. Other Thin Noses going to market with their kills or finds had stopped to watch the little show play out. A fireside storyteller couldn't do better. "It fell from the trees and died at my feet. A gift from the gods." He tried to screw up his slackened face into a scowl and nearly succeeded. "Try and take it and see what happens."

Gaunt spat into the pine needles. "You're slow. You always were." He had a short stabbing spear in a sling on his belt, and drew it out with a flourish. "The Gods mean for me to have it. Why else would they put it in my path?"

That's when they both noticed me.

I had emerged from the trail, passing the mounted torches by the frog and fish ponds and reaching the growing crowd. They stepped aside—maybe from my Broadhead bulk. Maybe from the saber-tooth tiger's fang on the cord around my neck.

The fang that marked a Fang.

"Why do you put fire in your words?" I asked the question, though I knew the answer. Forcing my voice to stay low. The Thin Noses were scared of deep

5

voices, instead of the shrill way that Broadheads sounded when we got excited. I'd lived amongst them long enough to know that.

Squint Eye and Gaunt stared at me—but their courage stayed.

I tapped the fang on my chest. "You speak hatefully in the Heap. You put fire in your words. The Tooth King doesn't like that." I nodded toward the monkey, and the two men who argued over it. "Tell me why."

"This monkey fell from that bough, Red." Squint Eye walked toward me, still bearing his little axe. "Into my path. It belongs to me. I'm going to make new gloves from its pelt. I need them. Need to keep my fingers warm." If he had any thoughts about a Broadhead telling him what to do, he kept them to himself.

"Go to the caves halfway up the Heap. We'll keep you warm." I gave him my best smile. Would a broad grin under a broad nose and thick forehead make him happy? I didn't know. "The Tooth King looks after everyone in the Heap."

"I was a hunter." Squints mumbled his words. "I shouldn't have to—have to huddle before a fire like an orphan. Or a cripple."

"You *are* a cripple." Gaunt had crouched low, his muscles tensing up under his sloth-skin coat. A wolf preparing to spring at prey. "And that monkey's mine."

He lunged for it—his hand jabbing out and grabbing the tail. He pulled the monkey closer to him, holding it to his chest. He would have made it up the slope, maybe toward whatever cave he called home, but my foot reached him first. The Hill Spirits gave Broadheads thick limbs, with lots of weight. A kick with all my strength would kill him—so I put half of it against his backside.

It wrecked his balance. Sent him stumbling on the ground. He rolled over and dropped the monkey as I closed in. The dead monkey rolled on the ground and lay there.

"It's mine!" Gaunt wailed.

"Mine!" cried Squint Eye.

They were both wrong. If you stole from a Fang, it was like stealing from the Tooth King. And if you stole from the Tooth King, you lost fingers or hands or arms. That was his law.

"Don't." I walked closer to Gaunt, clicking the bottom of my spear against the soil.

He squirmed back. Since he had attacked me, it was within my right to put a spear through him. But the Thin Noses feared Broadheads enough already—feared and hated. Because we were bulkier, shorter, stronger, and lived in a different way than them. I didn't wish to make the Thin Noses watching more afraid than I had to. No need to give them another story of the bloodthirsty Broadhead.

Instead, I spun the spear around. I drove the point into the soil—right between his legs. He winced and started shivering.

He would not be a problem anymore.

But Squints would. He darted out and grabbed for the monkey. A hungry man, and hungry men are desperate. I put my hand up. Let him run into my palm and shoved him back. Then I lunged down and grabbed the monkey by the tail.

His axe was out, his anger raised. "Broadhead beast!"

I swung the monkey by the tail. Bashed dead fur and dead flesh against his face. He gasped and stumbled. A push put him onto the ground. Next to Gaunt. Gasps from the assembled crowd. The Thin Noses enjoyed seeing the only Broadhead Fang in the Heap work.

But they needed to see some mercy too.

I hoisted up the monkey. "You both want this?"

"Yes." Gaunt clapped his hands. "Please, Red. I would fry it over my fire. I'll give you a piece. Broadheads eat a lot, don't they?"

"I have better things to eat." I pointed to Squints as I dropped the monkey and took the flint knife from my belt. "And you—you want it too?"

"I need the fur. I need gloves."

"You can make one glove." I started cutting. The knife worked, with some effort. Bones broke and the flesh gave way. Soon enough, I had the monkey in two pieces. I kicked the bottom half toward Gaunt and the top half toward Squints. Maybe that would make them happy.

They sat up, rubbing their injuries and grumbling. Gaunt smiled big and bowed. "Thank you, Red. A good Fang. A wise Fang. You are the teeth in the mouth of the Heap. You are the Tooth King's chosen. Glory! Glory to the Tooth King and to all the—"

I snatched up the spear and spun it about. Let the point face them. "You attacked a Fang."

"Ah." He opened and closed his mouth. "The Gods made me crazy. I wasn't thinking—"

"I will take one tooth from you."

"What?" Squints snarled. "One tooth? For a tooth, I could buy two monkey pelts!"

Buying and selling—another of the Tooth King's inventions. Part of what made the Heap real. What turned us from a collection of caves on a stony mountain into something else: a city. And in this city called the Heap, teeth mattered a lot.

"Hah!" Squints laughed. He tapped his sunken cheek. "Drink my piss, Gaunt. Pay what you owe!"

"You tried to steal from me, Squints." I grunted. "You must pay too."

That drained away his happiness.

Squints shuddered. "Red, I don't—I don't have many teeth left. I need what I have—"

I pointed to the pouch on his belt. The same pouch that everyone in the Heap wore—apart from youngsters. "I take it from that." My finger went up, going to his mouth. "Or I take it from that."

He and Gaunt exchanged a look. Then they reached into their pouches and took out one tooth each. I accepted the teeth. Yellow, curled up, the edges jagged. Human teeth. Chipped and marked with knives, to test that they were true teeth and not forged from chunks of yellow stone. I put them both in my pouch. Payment for the job of a Fang.

Thin Nose ways were strange.

"Good." I pointed to the monkey halves. "Take it and go."

They picked up the pieces and walked away.

The others stared and watched. Clutching their pelts or baskets of gathered roots or berries to take up to the market. Wondering what the Broadhead would do next, the way I would watch a big bear or sloth when I was little. Amazed at the danger and the size.

I gave them my best smile. "Go to the market—go and enjoy the Heap."

They turned away and resumed their journey. Muttering to each other. A tall woman in a shell necklace clutched her child's hand as the boy gripped a berry basket. "Broadhead brute. The King's pet beast." Murmuring those hateful words. Another Thin Nose quirk. Broadheads didn't gossip or talk about you behind your back. Perhaps I had grown used it.

Perhaps not.

Feet crunched on the pine needles behind. I turned about, letting the spear rest on my shoulder. "Red—there you are." It was Star. She bore the fang too, and the same mammoth fur cloak that I did, along with a broad-brimmed straw hat for the sun. "Were they giving you trouble?"

I stroked my beard, curling and red, like my hair, and tried to look wise. "I think I gave more trouble to them."

"You could have hurt them. They put fire in their words when they talk to a Fang, you can break a few bones."

"I am kind and good. Like Good Wolf to her pups."

She chuckled at that. "You and Good Wolf. You're certainly as hairy as her." Then she hesitated. "But I didn't find you to talk about pets." Using a new word—the word for what Good Wolf was. "There's trouble for us too. A dead man."

"Oh no." A death—the work of the Night Demons. "Where? Who?"

"We don't know who. The fisher women found him by the Blood River. They saw him there and sent a girl up to find a Fang. She found me, and now I have found you. We have to go and see this dead man."

I mumbled a few words to the Hill Spirits, under my breath. They were simple beings, unlike the complicated gods of the Heap, with their long names and complex roles and jobs. The Spirits liked Broadheads and looked after us, after they had fashioned us from stones and dirt and twigs. But they could be cruel too. Why else would they let us die?

The Hill Spirits made Broadheads, but the Tooth King had made Fangs. And dealing with death—collecting bodies and seeing what had killed them—was a job for Fangs.

"We do." I offered my hand and she clasped it. "Let's go to him."

We started down the slope, away from the Heap and its warm fire and large crowd. A hitch in my step pained me, but I ignored it. Bigger problems waited. Death could come here, but it seemed rawer and more powerful in the wilderness, amongst the trees and the rushing river. Like death belonged there. But so did we.

And we would see what death had done today.

The Blood River flowed from the Bloodwood and next to the Heap. Red stones and red soil below the water, which gave it its name. Red trees surrounded it, which gave the Bloodwood its name. And the river gave us fish and water, while the trees gave us wood and game. Broadheads could have lived in a place of plenty like that for a thousand seasons and not change it—but the Thin Noses had worked hard. Huts dotted the bank. Nets and fishing traps in the shallows. They had cut at the trees, leaving stumps and fallen logs all along the grass and the pine needles. Making it into a place of homes and Thin Noses, like the Heap itself.

A strange world. A twisted world. Like the reflection in a calm pond suddenly disturbed by a thrown rock. It did not belong.

A half-dozen fisher women stood on the bank, in a sobbing row. Their bare feet rested on stones washed smooth by water, and tears ran along their cheeks. Across from them, legs on the stones and the rest in the shallows, lay a body.

The dead man.

His face was up, his arms twisted. If he had bled, the current had carried away the blood. He wore a cloak and vest of black fur, now soggy and twisted by the river.

"Why?" The eldest of the fisher women dropped to her knees. "Another of us—gone! Taken up by the Rider. Carried away from his children, from those he loves!"

The others keened too.

I sucked in breath. Death could happen in a thousand ways in the Heap. Accidents or illness killed us. Beasts killed us. Sometimes, we died in amusing ways. We killed in battle. The Eaters captured and ate people from the Heap, and their bodies went into bellies. Occasionally, death came as a mystery. People would die, without sickness and with no mark on their bodies. The breath just stopped filling their lungs.

But each time, each death, was a sadness.

The Heap was the biggest collection of homes in the world. It had perhaps a hundred people—and everyone knew everyone else. And whenever someone died, we all felt it.

"Go and talk to them." I shuddered, as a keening wail crept up my chest. I looked at my feet. "You're better with talking."

"Thank you. I never really considered that." Star shrugged. "And you go to the dead man. That's what you want?"

"That's a Fang's job." I patted her shoulder and walked over.

The first thing to do was get him out of the water. I took hold of his ankles and pulled. Water in his cloak made him heavy. We would have to dry him off before burying him under the stones. I got him out of the shallows and onto the bank, and smoothed back his cloak. Black cave lion fur. Silky and good. Better than my mammoth fur cloak, and with a cost to match. He had not been a poor man.

I brushed hair from his face. Big cheeks and big eyes, white and staring and dead now.

"Frog Face." I knew him. I had seen him at the Cook Cave. We'd even eaten together. Munching on deer ribs—a much bigger pile of ribs in front of me than in front of him. He'd laughed about my appetite and mentioned how he needed to arrange more hunting trips, just to catch enough game to feed me.

Now, I added my voice to the keening chorus. I shuddered and sat on the ground. Frog Face would never joke again. He would never swing up his young daughter, Little Frog, into the air and catch her, or kiss his mate and nuzzle her. He was another soul taken by the Hill Spirits, and he'd dance with them in the mist and the clouds forever.

I dried my eyes. Stop the sadness. Be a Fang. See what killed him.

A crocodile. That was my first thought. He had been walking along the shore for some reason and the crocodile had come up and bit him and dragged him in. But if the crocodile killed him, why had he left him here? Why not drag him down and eat him? The same with any other beast. A tiger or cave lion would have carried him away to feed their cubs. And yet, Frog Face lay there.

A beast had not killed this man.

He not died long ago either. Probably it was in the hours before dawn that he had died. Otherwise, the animals would have dragged his body away or at least gnawed his flesh until the bones showed. But, apart from the water, he was whole.

So a beast had not killed him. Was it illness? Had some disease stopped the beating of his heart or prevented his lungs from filling with air, and he had just dropped into the water and lay there, bathed by the stream until the fisher women found him after dawn?

Perhaps.

Then there was the other possibility. That a man had killed him. The Thin Noses had their own words for that, when a man killed another, but not in a fight or a battle.

Wrong Death.

Star walked over. She had no spear, but another weapon—a stranger weapon—on a woven cloth scabbard on her back. She drew it out, keeping it in the scabbard, and jabbed the pouch on Frog Face's belt. It clicked. I opened up the pouch and looked inside.

Full of teeth.

"He was a rich man," I said.

"Very rich." Star agreed. "And a friend of Gummy's."

Gummy—the richest man in the Heap. Apart from the Tooth King, perhaps.

"A beast didn't do this." I patted the pouch. "It could be the Wrong Death. It could be. But not for the taking of teeth. If it was, they would have taken the pouch. But they left it here, full of teeth. So maybe it wasn't the Wrong Death at all."

"Or, it was not a killing from greed," Star said. "But from something else."

I was afraid of that. "Did the fisher women see anything?"

"They found the body when they arrived with their nets and spears." She pointed with the scabbard at the river bank. "Look there, in the mud."

Footprints. Dents in the soil, already fading. They went from the edge of the forest, to hardened earth and fallen pine needles, to the river bank, and then back under the trees—where they vanished.

I wiped tears on the sleeve of my cloak. "So, Frog Face walked down here and died…"

"No—there's only one pair." Star shook her head. "Think about it. Frog Face didn't walk down here." She moved back, setting her feet in the muck. "Look how small the marks are. Look how big the marks are here." Star motioned to the first set of footprints, coming down from the forest."

I grunted. "I see. But why do you ask me to look?"

Star sighed. "Frog Face was carried. The killer carried him, hauling him on his back. That's what made these marks deep." She motioned to the second set. "And these marks are light. His killer—the one who gave him the Wrong Death—brought him to the river bank, tossed him here, and walked away. Back into the woods."

It made sense. Heavier forces made deeper marks.

"You are very clever, Star." I shook my head. "But why do you say 'killer?' We have footprints, some deeper than others, and a dead body. We do not know any more than that."

She paused for a moment and took off her broad straw hat, revealing a head shaved clean. Star looked up at the body and cocked her head. "Why is his mouth like that? Half-open? The cheeks bulging, making him look even more like a frog. Or a chipmunk." She moved closer. "What's in his mouth?"

I leaned over and touched his chin. Cold flesh, and wet. Like a fish's skin without the scales. Just as she said, his mouth lay open.

Inside, it had been stuffed with soil. Rich, red dirt. Packed against his cheeks and covering his teeth. Obscuring his tongue completely.

I drew out a pinch of dirt and let it fall into the water. The stream carried it away.

No animal would fill a dead man's mouth with dirt. No disease would fill a dead man's mouth with dirt. Narrow Face hands alone would do that.

"He was killed," I said.

"Wrong Death," Star added.

I sat up and looked at the sky. It had gone gray. The seasons were turning. Fall giving way into winter. The regular way the seasons changed. But a Wrong Death placed here amongst woods transformed and broken by the Thin Noses—that was not regular.

And it made the cold bite harder.

After seeing Frog Face, dead in the water, I needed time away from the Wrong Death. I carried the body halfway up the hill, dead flesh on my shoulder, before letting Star and the other Fangs take it the rest of the way. They would bring it to the Cave of the Gods, where the shamans would bless it and prepare it for burial in the way of the Thin Noses. Good treatment for a body, who wasn't alive to enjoy it. A Thin Nose tradition. When a Broadhead died, we put them in the dirt with trinkets and good words, set the stones on them, and that was all.

Better to focus on the living.

I left them to their grim job and returned to the Heap—and then to the cave I called home. It rested halfway up the Heap, many, many steps away from the places where the Tooth King and the rich dwelled. But not near the bottom either. And not near the dark tunnels where the toothless—the ones who had only the teeth in their mouths—survived.

One such toothless girl greeted me as I pulled aside the hide flap and entered. "Red—you're back early." Mouse had been feeding jerky to Good Wolf and her pups, who sat obediently in a semi-circle in front of her. "How was the Fang's work? Break many bones?" She tossed the chunks of jerky. The wolves lunged up, snapping them out of the air. Muscle and sharp teeth doing their job. The chunks of meat vanished.

I crossed the cave floor, passing the fat lamps set on shelves on the wall, and settled next to Good Wolf. All the rules the pups had learned vanished. They scrambled over my lap. Their tails wiggled madly as they let out squeaks and whines. I settled on my back and let them crawl over me. So much life, after being so close to the Wrong Death. It felt nice.

"Red?" Mouse looked down at me. She was perhaps ten or eleven winters old, with golden hair framing a face like snow. Scrawny as a starved squirrel. "You seem sad?"

"There was a dead man near the edge of the river." I sat up as Good Wolf trotted over. "Given the Wrong Death." Should I tell her about the dirt stuffing his mouth? Probably not. It might frighten her.

Though there wasn't much that would frighten Mouse.

"The Rider will carry his soul up to the clouds." She motioned to the ceiling of the cave.

I scratched Good Wolf behind the ears. Her favorite place. She made a low humming noise. "I think I need to see Mother Rat. She might know something of it. The dead man was killed in the Bloodwood, or maybe the Heap, and carried to the river. His spirit left his body amongst the trees, or maybe in the caves."

Mouse folded her arms. "You think Mother Rat would know about killing?"

When I stopped scratching, Good Wolf jabbed at me with her paws—demanding more. I gave her the pets. "Mother Rat knows about everything."

"Hah!" Mouse let out a little giggle. "She'd like to hear you say that." She went to the cave mouth. "I'll go tell her, then. When do you think you'll be at her cave?"

"Sundown." That sounded likely. "You tell and you come back." I sat up. "You need to watch them for the rest of the day."

"For two teeth, I will."

That was Mouse—orphan turned bargainer. "One tooth every six sunrises."

"Two teeth." She tapped her toes—bare, even in the cold—on the mammoth fur rug.

"One tooth, and you can eat all the jerky you want and drink from my jug, and take some of those back to the rat caves." I pointed to the ivory figurines up on the shelf, mingling with the fat lamps. I had a good collection. A mammoth, a rhino, a pair of wolves, and a chunky figure that could be a Thin Nose, but I was sure was a Broadhead. "Mother Rat's children can play with them. But you must bring them back."

Mouse smiled. "Give me some jerky now."

I stood up and went to the highest shelf at the back of the cave. Out of reach of the wolves. I snatched up a good chunk of dried and spiced deer meat and dropped it into her hand. "Chew it on the way down. Thin Nose chatter bothers me."

"Then why do you stay in the Heap?"

"Some days, I am confused about that myself." I patted her head. "Go."

She scampered away, leaving me and my wolves in peace.

I went to the back of the cave and settled on a little stool. More jerky for me, washed down with something new: the juice of fermented melons, kept in a clay jug painted in elaborate yellow dots and blue stripes. I sipped. The liquid went bitter down my throat and burned in my belly. If I drank too much, I'd be drunk. Two sips were enough. I put the lid back on, set it on the shelf, and played with Good Wolf and her cubs.

Thin Noses had done so many magical things. Maybe the Hill Spirits made them out of gold or sunlight or mist, when they made us out of stone and dirt. Or maybe the Narrow People had the magic inside of them. But somehow, they had taken wolves and made them obey.

And I heard about other animals too. Rumors that goats or even cows—out on Bull Island—would do what humans wanted them to.

It had to be magic, and it was a magic that I loved. I'd purchased Good Wolf with some of the first teeth I'd earned. She grew fat with puppies, and I'd had a shaman oversee the birthing. Now, I had the full family. Perhaps someday, I'd raise more. Take in other wolves that wandered alone, without a pack. The strays who scavenged in the ashes of the Heap's cook fires, unwanted by everyone else.

That was what I had been, after all.

Good Wolf corralled her pups and pushed them back. Letting them sit in a yipping crowd near the corner of the cave. "You want more treats?" I took down some jerky for them and more for me. "You need jerky and the Thin Noses need teeth." I tossed food to the wolves and shoved some into my own mouth. A sharp tang. I'd bought this in the Cook Cave, and they'd treated it with fruit juice, to give a nice spice. I chewed and chewed and ate more.

The Hill Spirits gave the Broadheads big bellies, and we needed to fill them.

To do that, we hunted and gathered. I'd joined in the hunts for mammoth, bison, rhino, and bear. It was violent work, and put an ache in your bones and made your soul heavy. Fighting men was a different story, but we did it too. My father had been a warrior. He'd fought the Frost People when they moved south, and he had five notches on his clubs for the five skulls he'd smashed. Sometimes, he would tell me about it when he stared into the fire. Broadhead warriors killed in battle. It was what we did.

But killing like this? Giving the Wrong Death to a good person like Frog Face, and dragging his body out to the river? Stuffing his mouth with dirt? No Broadhead would do anything like that.

The wolves started making their calls—little howls from the pups. Good Wolf let out growls and whines and dashed to the door. I grunted and clapped my hands. Good Wolf, at least, quieted down.

Star pulled back the tent flap. "We've got Frog Face over in the Cave of the Gods. We need you, Red."

"I'd rather stay here." I took another bite of jerky.

"Among such good friends?" Star stared at Good Wolf, who looked back and tented her ears. "Who could blame you? But you have to do your job. The shamans are at work, and they might find out more. Bug Eyes will be there—"

"Bug Eyes." I groaned as I swallowed jerky. "His mind is broken. I think it's because he eats too many mushrooms."

"Shamans need the mushrooms. It lets them leave their bodies. Fly in the clouds with the birds or run with the deer. Travel down from the sky on lightning bolts. Run with wolves over the snow." She pointed at me. "Maybe your heart is full of envy. Closest you get to wolves are these ones right here."

"Bug Eyes flies through dung with flies." I stood and swept up my spear.

"He's good at his job, at least."

"His job asks him to be crazy. He's good at being crazy." I motioned to Star. "Lead the way."

We left my cave and headed up. Mouse would be here soon, to look after Good Wolf and her pups. She'd play with them, feed them, or put on their leads and take them up and down the Heap. I'd seen her: a little girl with a pack of wolves on leads, struggling against their strength. It brought happiness to many faces to see something so ridiculous.

Now, Star and I were going to see something bad.

The Cave of the Gods waited for us, further up the Heap. Over the seasons, the Narrow Ones had set up steps of wood and stone, to make the journey easier. More magic—building into the mountainside. We took these pathways. Ropes and platforms dangled from above. Platforms and ladders, so you walk up the Heap or climb it. More fires for the growing cold, and carved statues.

Mammoths reared high and trumpeting. Giant birds with their wings spread. Big apes and pouncing tigers. All carved in wood or stone, mounted with antler and bone, or set with garlands of flowers. Many more of them waited further up, to the top of the Heap. Where the Tooth King had his home, and the richest of the Heap dwelled. The statues and gardens that the Tooth King kept were for decoration. Beautiful things, kept because they were beautiful.

But outside the Cave of the Gods, the statues were holy.

The Narrow One Gods waited in a line by the entrance to the first of the caves. All of them, in ivory and wood, with flowers and fires and offerings by their elaborate shrines. The Thunder Snake, Monkey Boy, the Elephant Mother—and more as well. Gods to the wind and the rain, cleverness, and kindness. And at the end, a deer's skull without antler, peeking out from a blanket made from white wolf fur. The Rider. The God of death. Already, he had heaps of flowers and other offerings around his shrine, along with a weeping family. Frog Face's family, hoping that he would be carried by the Rider into the afterlife.

I glanced at Star. "Do you want to pray?"

"These aren't my temples." She shrugged. "Mine are further south, in my home." Sometimes, I forgot. Star was as much an outsider as me. "Let's go. Bug Eyes is waiting." She pointed to the cave mouth.

"Don't remind me."

I followed her down a stone path and into a wide chamber, where the shamans readied the dead. They had a stone table, with flowers along the edges. Masks hung from a wall alive with cave paintings. For a moment, my eyes went to those images. So much more vibrant, the colors bolder, than anything the Hillmen could make. Mammoth herds traveled across the ice. Hunters stalked their prey in the woods, while spirals of suns shone in gold from above.

And in the paintings there were the shamans, with the antlered heads of deer or the beaked heads of birds. Given all the intelligence of men and the power of animals, combined in one being.

Shamans always did have a high opinion of themselves.

A quartet of them, masked, worked on Frog Face's body. They had stripped away his cloak and wafted smoke from pleasing smelling herbs over his naked form. Some of them chanted. Other dabbed at his body from jugs of sweet juices. Star and I stood to the side and watched them work for a few moments.

One shaman broke away and trotted over to us. He had a mask like an insect's face, with carved mandibles and wild designs painted on the wood. He raised it, revealing a face covered in stubble. He stank too. Perhaps this shaman spent so much time flying over the tops of trees that he forgot to bathe.

"What—what is it?" Bug Eyes had a slurred voice, and stepped closer to me, his tongue hanging over his chin. "You have come for his soul, perhaps. Yes—yes, the Rider sent you. You'll carry him to the clouds, or under the earth." He clutched his fingers. "Or maybe you've come for me. Is that what this is?"

I grunted. "It's Red and Star, Bug. The Fangs."

"Oh—oh, yes. Just our two Fangs. They just look a little strange, that's it."

"He looks strange." Star pointed to me. "I look beautiful."

"I can't argue with that," I agreed.

Bug Eyes settled on his haunches and caught his breath. "Well, I could be forgiven. Yes, I must be forgiven. There's a buzzing in my head, you see. Buzzing—buzzing—it never quiets." He waved his hands in front of his face. Swatting invisible insects.

"Is that truth?" I asked.

"So many, many thoughts!" He snapped his fingers. "Why does water fall from the sky and not spit up from the ground? Why do men walk on two legs instead of four?" He motioned back to the shamans. "And why would a wealthy man, with a pouch and a mouth full of teeth, like Frog Face die face down in the river?"

"Maybe you could tell us." Star pointed to the body. "What did you find?"

"Ah—come and see." He pushed a shaman in a bird mask aside and clapped his hands.

We walked closer.

Bug Eyes pointed to the side of Frog Face's chest. "Do you see there? A wound. The redness all around."

I could see it. The mark bright against Frog Face's pink skin. Right below the ribs. The gash went out, crossing skin, growing small, and then vanishing. A painful red. No animal's claw or fang could have done this. A knife of some kind left the mark, driven in possibly from behind or the side, and pushed through. Or maybe a spear point.

More proof of the Wrong Death.

"And there is more." Bug Eyes hopped his way around, pushing aside the priests and chattering to himself. "Look here—and here!"

More scars. All like the first.

Star covered her mouth with her hand. "Three times. He was stabbed three times."

"Then his killer picked him up, took him to the river, and tossed him into the dirt." I scratched my nose. "He filled Frog Face's mouth with soil and left him there. Not so deep that the Blood River would carry him away. But why would he do that?"

"Why would he do that?" Star asked. "He wanted Frog Face to be found. And that's the 'why' I cannot answer."

Bug Eyes jammed a finger into his nose and worked furiously. "You're the Fangs, aren't you? Don't the Gods want you to find killers and bring them the Tooth King's justice?"

In this case, that meant death. If you killed in the Heap, you died.

"It makes no sense at all." Star settled on a stool. A shaman in a tiger mask moved in front of her with bone needle and leather strands, to stitch up the wounds. Frog Face would go whole into the ground. "But there's many things in this world that do not."

"Many Narrow One things," I added.

"Ah yes. Wisdom from our Broadhead cousin." Bug Eyes went to a little table, where tools rested in a neat row. "There is something else, big one. Something both of you should see. Another twist to the joke of Frog Face's death." He picked up a fur bundle and hopped closer to Star and I. "I found *this* in the dirt. In his mouth."

We looked at what rested in the bundle.

A single seed. Round and small.

Star picked it up and sniffed it. "A seed. Planted in the soil."

"In a dead man's mouth," I added. "It wouldn't grow."

Bug Eyes bobbed his head. "Very smart, Broadhead. Oh, you're a very smart Broadhead. Yes, yes, yes." I had an urge to rip off his mask, pick him up, and toss him somewhere into the back of his cave. "Let me ask you this: when we dress as wolves for the New Moon Dances, do we really sprout fur? When we

"Three times. He was stabbed three times."

carry a torch up to the peak of the Heap during the Night of Darkness, do we really bring back the sun? No—it's ritual. A symbol. And through symbols we touch the Gods." He pointed to the seed. "Perhaps that's what this is."

I had no idea what he was talking about.

"Ritual." Star took the seed and put it in her pouch—with her teeth. "A priest who kills, who drops a body by the river, and who conducts rituals with dirt and seed. That's who we're looking for." She groaned. "If a crocodile had gotten him, it would be easier."

"Perhaps it would have been a more painful death, if a crocodile had gotten him," I said—but she was saying something without really meaning it. Another confusing tradition of the Thin Noses.

But there was no more time to talk about crocodiles and men. A drumming came from the mouth of the cave. A low and slow beat, like the steps of a great creature. The shamans left the side of Frog Face's body. They formed a line by the entrance of the door and began bowing their heads—pressing their masked faces to the stone while they whispered a hundred different prayers.

"He's here!" Bug Eyes clapped his hands and joined them. "Glory!" He called out the word as he threw his whole body into the bow. "Glory to the Tooth King!"

Star and I exchanged a glance. We started bowing as well.

The Feathers came first—the Tooth King's personal guard. They wore cloaks of colorful feathers, with more feathers in their wicker hats and set along the tips of their spears and axes. They formed two lines by the cave mouth. Next came some drummers and finally, borne aloft on an elaborately carved litter held by slaves, the Tooth King himself arrived.

This was the man who had founded the Heap. He had decided that teeth could be used in exchange of pelts or vegetables or anything for trading, and turned a mountain of caves into a place where traders from Bull Island or the Mountains could come with their treasures.

He had taken me in, and made me a Fang.

Now, he clapped his hands and the slaves, all bearing the ash mark on their foreheads or shoulders, stopped carrying the litter. Other rich Thin Noses strolled out past him and settled in a loose half-circle. They made the Gods' Cave crowded, with their fine fur, necklaces of teeth and shining stones, and sweet-smelling perfumes. The Tooth King clapped his hands again and the slaves set his litter down on the earth.

He pulled himself up with a grunt. The Tooth King had something that I had seen very rarely outside the Heap: fat. His belly bulged and he had thick cheeks. It meant he did not move much, and he never struggled for food. A double necklace, alternating teeth with shining stones, dangled over his chest.

He wore a cape from the fur of bright, speckled sloth fur, and a vest of sleek otter pelts. Studs had been worked into his hairless head and cheeks, so that he gleamed.

Like he was the shining stone dug up from the earth.

"Glory to the Tooth King!" Bug Eyes cried. "He has brought us out of the darkness and into the light. He is like a good mother, who holds close her children, and teaches them to walk and then to run. All the Gods look kindly upon the Tooth King and—"

The Tooth King ignored him. Instead, he walked past the line of shamans and headed straight for Frog Face's body. The King walked—or perhaps waddled—to the front of the table, so that he looked directly down on Frog Face's face. He rested his hands on the cheeks of Frog Face. Then, a sudden, keening wail left his lips.

It echoed through the God Cave.

"He had such a good voice. He would come into my caves, Gummy and some others, and we would talk of the future. And after, with fruit juice in our bellies, we would sing. And he always had the best voice." He patted Frog Face's forehead. "Go well, friend. Travel well into the afterlife."

For a moment, nobody said anything. The Tooth King, grieving? It was like watching the sun shed a tear.

The Tooth King spun around. He walked toward Star and me. "Ah. My Fangs. The Broadhead and the woman from the south. Child Who Catches Falling Stars and Red."

Star's true name. She nodded and so did I.

"Good. That puts fire into my heart. I am glad you will catch the one who did this. I will give them justice." He formed a pudgy hand into a fist. "So— who did this? Who will my Feathers take and give to their knives?"

I stared at Star and she stared at me. Who would tell her that we didn't know anything about the murderer, besides the fact that he was bizarre? Star spoke up. "We do not know who wielded the blade. Not yet." She held up the seed. "But we found dirt in Frog Face's mouth. And in that dirt, this."

"A seed." The Tooth King carefully picked it up.

"Do you know—do you know what sort of seed it is?" My voice went high now. Squeaking, like that of a Thin Nose child. Asking the Tooth King a question was like conversing with thunder and lightning. "Or—or anything about Frog Face? You were his friend. Was he worried? Afraid of anything?"

"He was busy. He worked hard for the Heap." The Tooth King examined the seed as he spoke. "You should seek Gummy. They worked together. Explorers and gatherers, finding the future." He held out the seed. I formed my hands into a cup and the Tooth King dropped the seed into it. "Gummy's in the Flowering

Fields. That's near the Stone Hills, is it not? Where you came from, Red?"

I nodded wordlessly.

"Oh, you were so scared, then. Weak and half-starved and soaked from the rain." He rested his hand on my shoulder. "And you, Child-Who-Catches-Falling-Stars, you were on the run from your family's enemies. Marauders, who had butchered your father. I took you in. All are welcome in the Heap. That's why we are the greatest tribe, the biggest tribe, in all the world. Now, I ask of you, find out who killed Frog Face. This monster, this demon, who puts dirt into a dead man's mouth. Let him face the Tooth King's justice." He sighed deeply—more tired than angry. "Do you understand?"

"We do," Star said.

"Glory," I stammered. "G-glory to the T-tooth—"

A sad smile split his plump face. "You don't need to say it." Then he walked back to his litter and scrambled aboard. He settled down, clapped his hands twice, and his slaves picked it up. The entire procession wound its way out of the cave mouth and back into the path outside. Back to the peak, where the Tooth King had his throne, and he could look over everything.

The shamans slowly stood and crept back to the body. They continued working on it and muttering their prayers.

Bug Eyes bounced over to us. "I'd rather be in a tiger's belly." He pointed to me and Star. "Then be you."

I gave him a push. He bounced against the wall, into a painting of a charging rhino and slid to the ground with a squawk. I faced Star. "Gummy, then."

"Out in the Flowering Fields." Star sighed. "Too late to go now. I'll get what we need for the journey." Any journey could be dangerous. Maybe, someday, the forest trails would be safe. But that wasn't what they were now. "And you—"

"I'll go and see Mother Rat."

She sighed. "Dangerous, down there. Mother Rat collects bones." She tapped the fang on my necklace. "She might end up collecting that too, if you're not careful."

"I'm always careful."

"That is a lie." She smiled sadly. "And you are a bad liar."

I shrugged. "We have to go see. I'll take the seed, too. Maybe she'll know something about it. Mother Rat knows as much as the Hill Spirits, about many things." I held out my hand and Star set the seed in my palm. "You can meet me there, if you're worried."

"Pull you out of the fire?" She shrugged. "It would not be the first time."

I grunted, patted her hand, and headed out. Already, it grew dark. Though that didn't mean much on the Heap. The torches and fires turned day into night, turning the stone paths, the ladders and ropes, and the slopes and walls into a shifting twilight world of dancing shadows. The statues of the gods of the Narrow Ones lost their features in the darkness, their shadows stretching out over their offerings.

Frog Face's family still gathered around the Rider. Weeping and placing flowers, baskets of berries, and even a few teeth on the altar. It was good to wail and cry and weep for the dead. My task was harder. I rested my spear on my shoulder and descended.

Down to the bottom of the Heap, where the mountain met the forest and the fields. A narrow pass led to the entrance of a wide cave, decorated with white sticks carved in the image of a giant, leering rat. Jagged chunks of wood formed the teeth, like the rat was about to devour me as I headed inside— which wasn't exactly wrong. Fangs didn't go down here often. If the Tooth King was the sun, then Mother Rat was the moon, and this was her world. I joined the few Thin Noses ambling their way in, my foot aching with each step.

A guard stopped me. A stoop-shouldered Rat's Child, wearing a ragged vest of rabbit pelts stitched together. He bore a short club marked with flint spikes, and jabbed it at my chest. "Leave your weapons."

"I'm going to see Mother Rat," I said. "Mouse said to expect me."

"Mouse could squeak all she wants." He smiled, revealing a few missing teeth. Had he lost them in the usual way? Or had he ripped them out to buy and sell? "You leave your weapons."

I didn't like it, but had no choice. I took my spear, let him look at the jagged stone point, and rested it carefully against the wall. I took out my club next and held it out. When he grabbed it, I grabbed for his arm and hands. Pressed his fingers against the wooden handle of the club, hard enough to make him yell. I wasn't a warrior, but the Hill Spirits made Broadheads strong, and I used that strength now.

I squeezed and he yelled. "If I come back and find them gone, I will be angry. Do you understand!"

"Yes!" He wailed. I let go.

"Be careful with my weapons." I held out my hands, as if for a giant embrace. "Can I go in?"

He stepped back and pointed, as he massaged his fingers. "Go."

I entered. Down a narrow hall and then into a bigger chamber, where

Mother Rat ruled over her family, and everyone else who had teeth to spend.

Fat lamps and torches danced along the walls, covered in profane, wild paintings. Musicians worked in adjacent chambers, hidden by curtains so that the gut-string harps, airy flutes, and drumming seemed to come from the air itself. Cushions and chairs formed little circles, where hunters, craftsmen, and gatherers in the Heap guzzled fermented fruit juice from reed straws. A few took mushrooms, stolen from the shamans, and gingerly set the pale, speckled morsels on their tongues.

In Mother Rat's world, no law existed but her own.

I settled at one table, folded my arms, and waited. One table of rangy hunters looked at me and burst into laughter. A few hunched over and grunted, waving their arms and odd angles—mimicking the way Broadheads look. I glowered back. I could break them all, one after the other. It would be easy. But if I started a fight, this would be for nothing.

A little hand tugged at my cloak. "She waits for you."

It belonged to a child, perhaps six or seven summers old. He had a mop of dirty red hair and wore a cape of stitched rat hides. Broadheads would never allow orphans like this to grow up alone. We were all the same family—the whole tribe. But Narrow Ones were different, and that left the Lost Ones to join up with Mother Rat. *She* became their tribe.

I stood. "Then you must be my guide."

He smiled shyly and darted off. I followed him, weaving through the men around their tables. I reached the hunters who had been laughing at me and gave their jug of fruit juice a shove. It spilled over, drenching a Thin Nose with a narrow bristly beard. He rose up, rasping out a snarl, but I had already walked on.

"Sorry." I grunted. "Broadhead clumsiness."

Then I followed the boy down another dark cave. The tunnel ceiling went low. He handled it well enough, but I had to hunch over. Rock scraped at my side. I hated it, but went on—right to the end.

A circular chamber, with a fire burning blue in the center. A hole somewhere above let the smoke escape. Mother Rat sat on a stool, warming herself by the blaze. She hardly looked at me, focusing instead on stretching her hands above the fire, letting the heat play over thin fingers. All around her, chunks of stolen wealth. A set of mammoth tusks, intricately carved. Antlers in a neat pile. The golden furs of monkeys from the east.

I drew a tooth from my pouch and tossed it to the boy. "Buy something warmer than rat skins." I waved him back to the tunnel. "Now go." He scampered away.

Mother Rat faced me. A few seasons younger than me, perhaps, with dark hair running down to her shoulders. A curling scar crossed her face, trickling down from her forehead, running past her cheek, and ending in her chin. She wore a dress and coat of fox fur, trimmed with sable pelts, a necklace bearing a rat's skull dangling below a carefully composed, impassive face.

But behind her dark eyes, her mind had to be racing. Scheming like her namesake.

"Mother Rat—it brings joy to my heart that you have agreed to talk to me." I put flowers in my words. "Mouse told you I would be here?"

"Mouse is a good girl. Loyal." She stood from the stool and walked around the fire, making the shadows dance over the wall. "And you are too. Loyal to the Tooth King. You used to be a wolf, and now you're a dog. Did he send you? Asking you to sniff around?"

"Don't put fire in your words." Keep calm. If I showed weakness, I'd never leave these caves. "I came by myself."

Mother Rat stalked closer to me—closer than a stranger should get. "You want to know about Frog Face. Someone dies in the Heap, the Rider picks up a soul and carries it to the sky, and you think Mother Rat had something to do with it." Her hand went up. "Did I put a knife into Frog Face? Did I order it?" Her finger tapped on my nose. "Is that what you think?"

"No—not that." Maybe paying her a compliment would help. "But there is little that goes on in the Heap that you don't know about."

She smiled—making her look young, like Mouse. "Thank you for putting honey into your words. But you speak a falsehood. I don't know who killed Frog Face."

"Maybe you know about this." I took the seed out of my pocket and dropped it into her hand.

Mother Rat examined the seed. She brought it to her nose and sniffed, then let it rest on her tongue for a few moments before spitting it out back into her palm. "Hmmm." I always had trouble telling what Narrow Ones were thinking. If a Broadhead was angry, they raged. If a Broadhead was sad, they cried. But with Thin Noses? You rarely knew. "I will ask you a question, Red." Mother Rat went to the back of the chamber, where a set of clay jugs rested on a shelf of bone. "Do you know why the Tooth King lets me stay? He has warriors and Fangs. He could drive me out, if he wanted. But he doesn't. Why?"

It was a good question. "I do not know."

"He keeps me around because I am useful to him. That's the only reason he lets anything happen—it is good for him." Mother Rat opened one jar and took out a mushroom. "He says robbery is bad. If you take, he takes your hand. That's his way—isn't it? But those are only words. The truth is that sometimes, some people need things to be stolen. And they need to know who does the stealing. But while I trust him—in some ways—I don't trust you." She held up the mushroom. Stolen from the shamans. Speckled and wrinkled up. Like something that would fall out of a wolf's behind. "Eat this and I'll tell you."

My tongue went dry. My belly ached. The mushrooms were for shamans only. The Tooth King's rules were clear about that. Magic infested each bite. They would lift you up and carry you away. Leave you like Bug Eyes—someone who talked to spirits that no one else could see, and would leave his body to tiptoe across clouds or swim at the bottom of rivers.

But Mother Rat knew something. She always did. I proved my loyalty to the Tooth King by keeping his law. I would prove my loyalty to Rat by eating.

I offered my hand. The mushroom went into my palm. Though it had been in a clay pot for a long time, it felt wet. A tiny organ, cut out of a beast's belly.

No point in wasting time.

I tossed the mushroom into my mouth and chewed.

Terribly bitter. I sputtered and coughed and settled on my haunches. The juice pressed against my tongue—a sour, musky taste. It stuck in my gums and in the gaps between my teeth. I swallowed and swallowed again.

"Take this." Mother Rat offered me water from a bowl. I tilted it up and drank. "What do you see, Red?"

I closed my eyes. They blurred, like they did when I first woke up and left the land of sleep, where Hill Spirits and Night Demons talked to me. But the blur remained. The stone walls stretched up, going far into the distance and I could not see the cavern ceiling. I tried to stay still. I looked at Mother Rat.

She had dark fur on her skin. A naked tail slipped out from behind her cloak. Curling about on the floor like a giant worm.

"You want to know about the seed?" She put her hands on my shoulders and leaned closer. Rat teeth projecting from her lips. "I stole it. One of my little mice stole it, and brought it to me. I have little mice all over. So when someone wants something stolen, they come to me. That's what he did—he came to the Rat Market, and bought it from me."

He? The one who had planted that seed in Frog Face's mouth?

"Who?" She'd know. Mother Rat knew all.

"That, I can't tell you." Mother Rat waved her hand. "And not because I don't want to. I don't know. He wore a mask."

A dark image appeared in the crevice by the painted wall. The outline of a man, hunched over—and cloaked. His face lost in a mask of shadow.

The mushrooms had done to me what they did to the shaman. Letting my mind see what my eyes could not.

"A mask made from the skull of one of the giant apes, who live far to the east, and a cloak as black as night."

Now, I could see him better. The ape skull, hiding his face from view. Bigger than a human head, and half hidden in the hood of his cloak. The pelt from some black-furred animal. A bear maybe, with a hood that put shadow over the bone. A shaman's mask? No. The skull belonged to the dead. A dead man, who had purchased the seed, and then gone out and brought the Wrong Death to Frog Face.

A Night Demon in the form of a man.

"He bought…the seed?" I managed to force the words out of lips that seemed frosted with icicles.

"He bought many seeds. They were just what he wanted. He knew where they came from."

This Night Demon, this spiller of innocent blood, gazed at me with fiery eyes.

"Where?"

"Gummy's expeditions. Out into the Flowering Fields. He's gathering seeds and a few ended up in my market. Why does Gummy gather seeds and not eat them? I don't know. But a man that rich in teeth can do what he wants."

And one had ended up in the Blood-Spiller's hands, and then in Frog Face's mouth.

The Blood-Spiller shrank back into the shadow.

Something else replaced him. Dark eyes. Big teeth. Emerging from the shadow. A monster, who lurked in the dark places of the earth and lived only to crunch bones and shred flesh. Or maybe that wasn't right. Maybe it was just another animal, just trying to live, until my father ordered a group of warriors to drive the cave bear from its den, so we could have it—and brought me along.

I walked toward the cave. The other Broadheads, the men of the Hills, walked with me. Torches burning, for bears feared fire, and spears raised—for anything was better than getting close enough to touch those claws. We walked through the mist, the cave mouth stretching above us, and I stumbled and tripped, and wished that I was away. Back by the warmth of my campfire, hearing the songs of old heroes.

Knowing that I was too scared.

My father glanced back at me. "Red?" My name, in a Hillman's voice. It made my legs weak. He saw that I was scared and his nostrils flared out. His voice going high—angry. "You're frightened." He put his hand on my shoulder. "I am headman. You are the headman's son. We'll go together. You cannot be scared."

We went up to the cave mouth. The bear, fat with the food it gobbled before its long sleep, emerged and filled the entrance. The roar came next, shaking the very world. Night Demons whispered in my ear and told me to run.

And I had. All the way to the Heap.

But this time, the bear burst out, glittering with stars and lost in shadow. It reached for me.

A hand caught my shoulder and pulled me back. Star's face. "Red?" She slapped my face. The sting made me blink, the pain sending the bear away. Star gleamed. She spun around and faced Mother Rat—who still bore fur and her rat's tail. "What did you do to him?"

"Nothing." She smiled with rat's teeth. "He did it all himself."

Her hand went to the scabbard at her back. She pulled free the weapon hidden there. The Lance of the Sky. A gleaming material, worked into the edges of a carved pole, placed into the wood. A fallen star, carved and forged by some strange magic. It caught the light of the torches and candles and gleamed, and it shone so bright that I had to close my eyes. Leaving the Night Demons to play around in the darkness that remained.

"Mushroom." I murmured. "She gave me one. Worth it—I learned—"

"Tell me later." She brandished the lance at Mother Rat, who squeaked and crawled back. Going small and slipping into a crack in the stone. "Come on."

We went outside, back through the Rat Cave. Star kept her lance at the ready, giving it a swing at anyone who came close. We made it through the front chamber and outside. The coolness, wonderful against my skin. Then Star brought me to a frog pond, one of many that dotted the outside of the Heap, and forced me down. She shoved my face into the cold water.

The chill warped through me. I coughed and struggled.

She hauled me up. I vomited. What was left of the mushroom sprayed out, staining the stones. A few Heap-dwellers watched, and pointed and laughed. Look at the Broadhead. Even as a Fang, he couldn't handle the Heap.

"The seeds." I looked up at Star, the bones still gone from my limbs. "Stolen from Gummy's expedition."

"And Frog Face was a friend of Gummy." She patted my shoulder. "We go tomorrow. We'll leave the Heap and ask Gummy himself about it."

"Yes. Good." I hesitated. "I ran, Star. I ran away from the cave bear."

She sighed and patted my shoulder. "You don't run anymore. And there's no one else I want at my side."

I tried to keep from vomiting again. We would leave the Heap at dawn.

CHAPTER TWO
FIRES GROW IN THE FLOWERING FIELDS

The next morning, with the sun faint and the Hill Spirits themselves just finishing their battle with the Night Demons, Star and I left the Heap and went to the Flowering Fields to find Gummy. A trail went through the

Bloodwood and then to the Fields, but there was much land to cover, and—to make it worse—Eater raiding parties sometimes snuck into our land to steal travelers from the path. A dangerous route, even if we weren't seeking a Narrow One who wore a skull and gave the Wrong Death.

We took Good Wolf. I let Mouse watch her puppies so that Good Wolf could watch after me.

My leg ached. I ignored the soreness and trudged on.

At least Good Wolf enjoyed the walk. She darted ahead of us, pausing to jab her nose into the grass on the side of the road or the bases of the trees, occasionally lunging to grab something interesting in her jaws and gnaw on it as she hurried along. Her tail went back and forth. Occasionally, she would glance back at Star and I, her mouth open and her tongue lolling, like she was wondering why we were not as happy as her.

It was easy to make a wolf happy.

"Good weather for walking." Star pointed to the clear sky. "But winter's on the way."

"Winter." I could feel it in my leg. Winter meant empty bellies and dead children.

"You'll face it in the Heap, Red. You've faced it before. How many winters have you spent in the Heap?"

I used my fingers to count. "Five."

"And how many times have you died?"

I glanced at my fingers—and found no answer there. "This must be Narrow Face humor, which I don't understand. I haven't died at all."

"And you won't die this time. That's the glory of the Heap. There are some things you just don't have to worry about."

In front of us, Good Wolf let out a howl. She padded back, not happy anymore—but wary. She moved protectively in front of Star and me, like we were her pups. And maybe, in a way, we were. Her fur stood up, her lips curling back to show teeth as her tail jabbed up and her legs went tense and stiff as dead branches. Get ready to strike.

"What is it?" Star asked, reaching for the Sky Lance.

But I smelled them, just after Good Wolf did.

Eaters.

Two of them walked out from the trees. Another two, stepping onto the trail behind us to complete the trap.

We all feared Eaters. Everything was prey to them, whether it walked on two legs or four. They were Narrow Ones, but while the people of the Heap had used their strange magic to make teeth valuable and build a new world out of the mountain, the Eaters used their magic to eat. They caught many going through the woods, dragged them away to their villages, and cooked and ate them.

And that wasn't all they did, for a body had more to it than just food. Each eater wore vests and ribbons of tanned human skin. Necklaces of fingers, toes, and ears dangled over their chests. Even their clubs and axes had the bones of men in their makings.

The Eater at the front, a big fellow with filed teeth and a cape of countless monkey pelts, made a little, casual humming noise to himself. It was like a sound a child would make when they spotted an interesting insect—right before they started to pull off its wings. He had a long club made from a leg bone, studded with sharp chunks of flint. A long knife, perfect for hacking at flesh, rested in his belt.

"Hello!" the bald Eater gave us a cheerful wave. "Look at this pair. From the Heap, yes?" He spoke the language of the Heap—the language of most Thin Noses—with a lilting, gentle voice. Like he was a friendly traveler.

"Walk away." Star drew out the Sky Lance. Sunlight glittered on the curves of shiny stone worked into the smooth, white wood. My breath left my mouth in a high-pitched Broadhead whimper. Star never took out the Lance of the Skies unless she was willing to use it. "Walk back into the woods and pretend you didn't see us. I won't ask you again."

"Pretty." The Eater smiled. "I will use that to pick out the pieces of you from my teeth."

He was right to be confident. The Eaters outnumbered us, even with Good Wolf. Two warriors could not defeat four, and I was not even a very good warrior. I had trouble counting very high, but I knew that. I had the strength and could probably kill one Eater, maybe two. Breaking them like twigs. But one Eater had a bow, an arrow at half-draw, and I couldn't break that.

The bald Eater nodded in our direction. "Put your pretty weapon in the dirt, along with the Broadhead's spear and club, and we'll take you back to our camp. Big Mouth will be glad." He motioned to me. "You're large. Our children will dine well for at least a week on your ribs alone."

I hefted the spear, squared my shoulders, and glared at him. If I spoke now, it would come out in a squeak. Better to be silent. To let my size make them afraid.

It didn't work.

One of the two from behind us walked closer. A thin Eater with a round belly and only a ragged loincloth for the cold. He pointed his spear at Good Wolf, who gave him a growl. "Stop your wolf from making noise!" He made a loud whine and covered one ear. "Her noises bother me! Stop them or I'll silence her for good."

I faced him and hoisted my own spear. "Don't touch her." The Eater next to their leader, who had a dried finger worked into the braids of his beard, raised his bow and pulled at the string. I didn't care. It put fire into my heart when they threatened Good Wolf.

She just kept growling.

"Why not?" The round-bellied Eater sneered. "I know what the Heap does to wolves. They took her hunter's heart."

I let out an angry squeak. Go with them? No. We had to fight, and trust to the Hill Spirits to let us win.

I rested my hand on Good Wolf's back. "She's not that tame." Then I clicked my tongue.

She leapt for him, jumping up and going for a weak spot, like her parents had done to deer or boar in the wilderness. Her jaws caught something, pulled, and ripped. Hard to make out what amongst the fur, thrashing limbs, and the screams, but blood jutted out from where his neck met his chest. Sometimes, I forgot that Good Wolf was actually a wolf. She always found a way to remind me.

Star ran to the Eater archer with the bow—her long legs pumping as she swung up her spear. He loosed his arrow a moment later. The hum hit the air—and thudded into the dirt between her feet. Her speed startled him,

But she didn't get a chance to reach him. Another Eater, a short Thin Nose with long, wild hair, slid into her path. He had two stone knives, long weapons with edges chipped to make them leave ragged scars, and spun them as his tongue slipped down and wetted the dead lips of his mask.

The Eater with the monkey-fur vest charged at me, before I could even raise the spear. His club hummed down, swung from the side with both hands. It slammed right into my gut and then I couldn't stand. The tops of the trees loomed above me, the sky bright. The Eater jumped on me, putting his knees in my chest, holding me in place.

"Little Knife—take the woman!" He bellowed the command as he swung up his club. I raised a hand and grabbed his wrist. I could hold him—until Good Wolf could reach me. I at least had the strength to do that.

"I got her." The archer had moved further back. "I'll put an arrow through that—"

His words ended in a little wheeze, followed by a guttural, wet sound. His bowstring twanged.

I twisted my head to the side to see. The archer stumbled back, a gash opened from his neck to his belly button and gushing out red. He stayed on his feet for a moment more before dropping.

Another man stood beside him—no, a Night Demon. He wore a cloak of woven raven feathers, which matched his black hair. Small too. Coming up only to my shoulder. But his weapon. That had to be a Night Demon's claw. A rectangular paddle of polished wood, covered in delicate carvings of bird wings and bird skulls. All around the edges, shining points of some black stone. I'd seen it, carved and worked into weapons that cost fistfuls of teeth. Far more than any Fang could afford.

Obsidian.

The Eater with the long hair stared at the newcomer in surprise. "Who—" Then Good Wolf sank her teeth into his leg, her jaws sinking low and drawing blood. He gasped as he dropped to one knee, and tried to catch my dog with his knives. Star put her lance into his throat first. She plunged it down, the blood spurted, and he dropped.

That left the Eater on me. Their leader. He stood up and faced this newcomer. "I'm a favorite of Big Mouth." He held his club near my face, close enough for the point of the flint to poke my nose. "He'll know you killed me. When he eats, the flesh takes him away. It makes him dance. When he dances, the spirits let him see anything. He'll know you killed me and he'll come for you."

The Night Demon had crossed to the center of the trail. His big club rested at his side. "Let him."

The Eater shrieked and charged. He hoisted his club high and opened his mouth for a battle cry.

The obsidian-edged club hummed through the air and caught him first—right in his open mouth. The sharp stone edges bit through his lips and cheeks and kept going, all the way into bone. They stayed there for a moment, and the Eater made a coughing, rasping noise. Then the Night Demon wrenched it free and struck again—and the Eater's head left its neck and fell away. It plopped into the dirt and his body followed.

Star stared at the Night Demon. "Raven."

"Star." Raven took a square of black panther fur from his cloak and began carefully cleaning his club. "You're a long way from your home."

"So are you." She walked over to me and offered her hand. "Red, are you harmed?"

It felt odd—a Thin Nose asking if I was harmed. Then again, I wasn't a warrior—and she was. "He stopped my breath, but it's back." I accepted her arm. "You know this Night Demon?"

"He's a man, strange as it may seem." She grinned. "From the Far Lands."

That place—the furthest lands there were. A bridge across the ocean had brought the Thin Noses there, to a place where Broadheads had never gone. A place without men of any kind and no spirits. Or maybe, the spirits were different. They would have to be, to make something like Raven. He smoothed back his hair and examined the bodies of the dead Eaters. He took the arrows

The Eater shrieked and charged.

from the quiver of the archer, put a knife in his belt, and snatched up an apple from an Eater's pouch as well. Then he tossed a dried ear to Good Wolf, who snapped it up and gnawed joyfully.

I snorted. "Don't give my dog a dead man's ear."

"Why not?" Raven asked. "They're not using it." He returned to his feet. "Don't worry. I'm not looking for you."

"Raven's a manhunter," Star explained. "People tell him to bring other people back, and that's what he does."

"Like a Fang," I said. "But he doesn't serve law."

"I serve whoever rewards me." He pointed back through the trees. "Right now, that's Gummy. We heard some Eater scouts might be lurking around, so he sent me to find them. It looks like they found you first." He gave the lead Eater's head a kick and sent it rolling into the shade of the trees beside the trail. "Now, their spirits have taken flight to the Land of Night. I'll hunt them there forever, when I join them."

"What?" What was he talking about?

"It's from the Far Lands," Star replied. "Well, we're looking for Gummy as well. Need to see him about a death in the Heap. Maybe you could introduce us?" She put her hands on her hips. "After chasing me for a few seasons, it's the least you could do."

"That was only a job—and it's over. So I don't see why not." He pointed to me. "Come along, Red. Gummy will want to see you."

Good Wolf pressed her head close to me. She made an excited humming and I worked the fur behind her ears and made cooing noise to let her know she had done good. Then her mouth opened. She dropped the dried ear, soggy with her spit now, into my hand.

The sun sat high in the clouds when we walked out of the Bloodwood and into the Flowering Fields. In the spring and the summer, they would be covered with sprays of brilliant blooms in the tall grass. Now, there was less of that. Bits of early frost added a shine to patches of grass, and many flowers had died—though many remained, and added brightness to the winter gray. Raven led us down the trail and along a stream that ran to the Blood River, now flowing fast with snowmelt, before coming to a little encampment.

Lean-tos and tents waited by the water, and a trio of campfires in rock pits burned and danced merrily. Plants had been arranged everywhere. Chopped stalks, bushels of flower petals, and bowl upon bowl of seeds. One bowl contained deep red seeds, another looked dark and shiny, and another had a green sheen to them. Maybe ten or fifteen Narrow Ones worked continuously. They hacked at plants, cut-up fruits, or took bowls of seeds and headed out over the cold soil.

Was this a ritual? Leaving offerings for the Narrow One Gods? I didn't like it. They were carving up plants like an animal's carcass.

Raven brought us to the side of the big campfire. I sat. My leg wanted the rest. "Gummy." Raven waved his hand to a scrawny figure seated on a fallen log, overlooking the fire. "Look what I found."

"Eh?" Gummy turned around. I had seen him before. Frog Face had introduced us. But it felt odd to be this close to one of the Heap's greatest residents—a man second only to the Tooth King. He had wrinkles worked into his tanned skin, and thinning hair in wild tufts. He smiled, showing that he had lost every tooth. "Two Fangs? Well, welcome. Come and join us. You're just in time for lunch."

Two slave children, maybe Mouse's age, sat across from him, their jaws working furiously. They spat together into a pair of bowls. I sniffed. Roast deer meat in one bowl, apple in the other. Now reduced to shapeless pulp. They handed over the bowls.

"Red—the Tooth King's Broadhead. And Star. Our visitor from the south." Gummy picked up the mush and gobbled it down. Chunks spilled over his chin. He wiped the stains clean on his arm. "Why are you here?"

I looked at Star. She gave me a quick nod. She'd tell him the news.

"Frog Face. The Rider has carried him away." She removed her broad-brimmed straw hat. "And it was the Wrong Death. Someone gave him the Wrong Death."

A moment of stillness on Gummy's face, with a mouth full of chewed food. For a moment, he was still as a cave painting. Then, he chewed once, and twice, and swallowed. He stood with a sigh. "That puts ice in my heart. I will weep for Frog Face. He was my friend. His teeth paid for much of this. Him, the Tooth King, and me—this is our work." He extended his skinny arms, indicating the encampment and the many bowls of seeds.

"And what are you doing here?" I asked, glancing at Raven.

He shrugged. "Don't ask me. I don't even understand it."

"Let's go for a walk. Your dog can stay here." Gummy motioned for us to follow as Good Wolf stretched out and lay down by the fire. One slave-child, his hair a tangle, reached out a nervous hand and smoothed down the fur on her back—she responded by rolling over and revealing her belly.

Gummy came to his feet with a grunt. "I'll take you to Autumn. You'll like her, Red. Her hair is close to yours!" He let out a happy cackle—but there wasn't much humor in it. Frog Face's death had made him more than sad. It made him flinch. He was scared.

We walked along to the edge of the river. Raven trailed after us, keeping a small amount of distance, but never letting Gummy out of his sight. He stood off to the side, a bit further down the stream, his feathered cloak wrapped around him like giant wings. I wondered if he would spread that cloak out and take flight.

A Thin Nose woman sat on the shore, filling up a clay jug with water. She was stout, with a tangle of reddish gold hair over a face spotted with numerous freckles. Not as red as mine, but red nonetheless. She wore a deerskin dress, covered in various belts, satchels, and pouches, and she tended to the seeds and the bowls of water with the same care that Good Wolf tended to her pups. She hardly noticed as we walked to the riverbank and stood across from her.

"Autumn." Gummy raised his voice. "Autumn!"

She perked up. "Gummy." She sprang up, bearing one basket. "Look here. Dirt and water, and the seed. And it doesn't grow. But here..." She motioned to a tiny sprout of green on the riverbank. "It does. So we need more dirt. Big amounts of dirt. Maybe a bigger basket. Or clay? Maybe that would work..." She cocked her head. "Who are these?"

"Two Fangs. The Broadhead's Red and the southerner is Star."

Autumn put her hands on her hips and squinted at me. "Yes. They have names. Most people do. But why are they bothering me when I'm working?"

"We need to know what you're working on," Star explained. This was odd. Usually, people in the Heap were eager to help Fangs—they knew what we could do with a single command. But Autumn was fearless. "Or are you too busy dipping seeds in water?"

"You don't understand. The Monkey Boy could fill your mind with pure intelligence and you still might not understand." She sighed as she knelt down and resumed filling the clay jug.

I took a step closer. I put flowers in my words. "You're right. We are foolish. I'm a big fool—that's very true. But maybe you could try your best to explain." I gave her a wide smile. "I will try my best to understand."

She gave me a quick smile back. "Yes." Then she sprang up and pointed to my belly. "What do you put in that?"

"Food?"

"What sort of food? Where does it come from? No—don't answer. I'll tell you. Meat and plants, from what's hunted and what's picked along the trails." She pointed to my belly. "You work hard and that fills you up. Until it doesn't.

What if you aren't lucky during a hunting expedition? Or there are no animals? Or you can't find any roots to dig up or fruit to pluck? What happens then?"

"I would starve."

"Yes, you would. And if things didn't change, the Rider would pick you up and carry you away." She reached down into one basket and drew out a single seed. The same sort that had been placed in Frog Face's mouth. "But it doesn't have to be like that. Do you know what this is?"

She must think I was truly stupid. "Ah—a seed."

"It's the future. You do know that where seeds are planted, plants grow, don't you?"

I had seen it happen. Squirrels buried seeds and forgot them. The next season, shoots would burst out of the earth and reach for the sun. Sometimes, the Heap people would scatter seeds and they'd do the same. It could help during lean times.

The Hill Spirits wanted it to be that way, so that's the way it was.

"What if *we* planted the seeds. Truly planted them." Autumn was nodding now, enjoying playing the storyteller. "We planted them, stayed in one spot, and waited until they grew. Then, we pluck the fruit or pull out the roots. We could eat them whenever we'd like. If we didn't want to be hungry, we would just plant more seeds ahead of time."

"Your mind is broken." Star tapped her skull. "There can't be that much control."

"There can be. I've been learning." She pointed to the river. "Water, sunlight, good soil. That's what the plants need. But you don't just put them in the dirt and forget about them. You have to tend to them, like you tend to your children. Until they're ready."

Control plants? Grow food? You might as well ask a mother bear to give you her milk. It would be magic.

Then again, I had seen much magic in the Heap.

Star rubbed her forehead. She walked past the riverbank and kicked at the water—sending up a spray. "Think about what you're suggesting. You know how much time that would take? You wouldn't hunt for a day, bring home a big kill for a few night's feasts. You'd have to work constantly. Pouring in the water. Tending the soil. Hoping they get enough sunlight. Scaring off animals who would try and eat the fruit before you could get it. And so many plants would die, or make only a little food."

"Maybe. But with planning and hard work, you could grow enough not to starve. Learn how the dirt works, how the water grows, and you could make a whole field of apples! You could feed yourself, and your family, and have so many left over. Give them to others. Invite more people to come in, or make more children. They could tend the apples. You know that each one has seeds, don't you?" She started talking faster, bouncing up and down on the balls of her feet. "Each seed could be many more apple trees, which would make more seeds. The Heap could change. So many more people could be there—all growing, and working, and happy." She reached over and rested her hand on my belly. "And this—this would never be empty again."

I froze up. Her fingers—which had been in the river—like icicles. Autumn froze as well. She stared at me and pulled her hand away.

"I don't know if that makes sense to you, Red."

Gummy let out a wheezing laugh. "It makes sense to me, lovely girl. It makes sense to the Tooth King too." He hesitated, the laughter dying on his lips. "And it made sense to Frog Face."

"Frog Face?" Autumn stared from Gummy to me and Star. "What happened?"

We had to tell her. I made a sort of gurgle. Like the noise Good Wolf made when she ate the wrong food and vomited.

Star put her hand on Autumn's shoulder. "Gone."

"Gone?" Autumn's mouth opened. Her eyes glimmered as she sank down to her knees.

"The Wrong Death," Star added.

"He believed in me. He believed in what we're doing here. Who could ever—who could do something like that? To give the Wrong Death to a good man like Frog Face?"

"We'll find out." I wanted to reassure her. Like my father and mother reassured me in the hills, when I was scared of the thunder or the rain. I tried to make my voice soft, to end the squeak in it. "We'll find who gave him the Wrong Death and he will face the Tooth King's justice. I make a promise with my heart."

Autumn accepted Star's hand, who helped her back to her feet. "I wish to help."

"And I'll help too." Gummy had settled onto the bank of the flowing stream, removing his furry boots to jab his feet in the water. He kicked them out now, sending a spray of cold water into the stones and rushes on the far shore. "Whatever you need."

Time to show them the seed. I took it from my pocket and gave it to Autumn. She held it up to Gummy. "Stolen, from your camp here by one of Mother Rat's little mice." I explained the details. "Then the one who gave Frog Face the wrong death, who spilled his blood, purchased it from Mother Rat. The Blood Spiller then put it into Frog Face's mouth, along with dirt."

"Planting it," Autumn said.

Star listened carefully, saying nothing.

"Why would he do that?"

Gummy offered his hand and Autumn dropped it into her open palm. He sniffed the seed. "My mind is empty. I have no answer." He gave it back to Star, who passed it to me. "Why would they do that?"

"Maybe the killer is a Night Demon," I suggested. "They would do something like that. They cause the scary dreams, you know. After the sun goes down."

"Maybe," Star said. "But I have another idea. It's like what Bug Eyes said. About how we build fires and make offerings. Rituals, to please the Gods. Maybe that's what this was. Putting a seed in Frog Face's mouth—a ritual to please a God."

"No God would want that," Autumn said.

"Not the ones we worship," Star replied. She walked closer to Gummy. Leaning in and staring at him. "But why the seed taken from here? He could have gotten any seed. They wait in the earth. They're in most fruits—as Autumn just said. Why take one from you?"

He put his weathered lips together, hiding the gums from view. His eyes flicked down to the grass and then back at Star. "I do not know."

"Who could?"

"The Tooth King." He let the words fall heavy—dragging them out. Letting us know the danger. We were just Fangs and the Tooth King was our king. "But there is another who might help."

"Who?" Star demanded.

Footsteps crunched on the grass of the riverbank. Raven had returned, a gatherer in a squirrel-fur hat standing next to him. Gummy came to his feet with a groan. "Raven—what now?"

"The band that went to the Moon Pools—they sent a messenger back." Raven patted the Narrow One with the squirrel hat. "They found some Broadheads."

Broadheads—what were once my people.

"Yes, Gummy—a camp of them." The squirrel-hatted Thin Nose bowed his head. "They were around one of the Moon Pools, getting water. A hunting party, with spears. They spotted us and made some noises, and we made some back. Then we went over to the hills, and that's where I left them. No one's raised a spear. No one's thrown a rock or shot an arrow. Not yet."

"Well, then the Elephant Mother has given us a gift, like a good mother should." Gummy clapped a hand on my shoulder. He was a scrawny, old man and weak—but his pat nearly made my legs buckle. "We have Red here. Go and talk to the other Broadheads. Explain to them that we're not here for war."

I swallowed. My voice went shrill. "What sort of Broadhead?"

"A Broadhead's a Broadhead," Squirrel Hat replied.

"Do they wear white fur or are they covered in rock dust?"

He shrugged. "I didn't see. And it's growing dim."

That could mean anything. The war could have already started. By the time I got there, words might have given way to spears and stones. And I wasn't a warrior.

Star had been listening. Now, she took a step closer to Gummy. "If we get the Broadheads to go away—if we keep peace between your gatherers and this hunting party—you'll tell us what we need to know." Not a question. An order.

Gummy gave a slow nod. "I will."

"Then Red and I will go." She looked back at the others. "Anyone else?"

"I will," Autumn said.

"You're certain?" Gummy motioned to the seeds. "There's danger amongst the Broadheads. They are big and brutal and strong." He glanced at me. "I apologize, Red. I put no fire in my words for you."

I didn't know what to say. They sounded fiery to me.

"I have to go," Autumn replied. "I have to explain to the Broadheads what I'm doing. Once they know, they'll understand that there's no need for war. We'll have so much food, we can trade what's left for more hides and horn and meat. Even more than we already do. Once they understand that, they won't want to fight."

Except that Autumn had explained it to me, and I didn't understand. Then again, the way Autumn talked was good. She filled her words with passion and courage. She believed in this magic—of planting seeds and tending the plants and growing food. She believed in it the way that people believed in Gods. And she seemed to fill everything she did with that same courage and belief.

Maybe she would convince the Broadheads.

Either way, I wanted to walk with her in the fields.

We left the encampment along the stream and headed further across the field, to the Moon Pools. Just three of us under the setting sun, if you didn't include Good Wolf—Star and I loping ahead and Autumn struggling to catch up. Good Wolf dashed around us, occasionally letting out a yip or chasing after some bug or mouse in the greenery. We crossed open patches of grass, tall and waving slight as a cold wind blew down from the darkening sky. Over to a set of hills, gentle ripples covered in blue grass. A herd of aurochs grazed in the distance, occasionally snorting or shaking their big heads.

Further on, we reached the Moon Pool. Star's long legs carried her ahead. She held up her hand and Autumn and I froze. Her hand went to the handle of the Lance of the Sky, while I gripped my spear with both hands. Autumn came up behind us as Good Wolf crouched down, ready to hunt.

Up ahead, a cluster of Broadhead men and women rested around a small campfire, bright against the dying light. They huddled in the thick pelts of bears, mammoth, and rhinos, spears and heavy clubs leaning on their shoulders. Gray dust on much of their clothes.

Hill Clan. My clan.

I stared at their clothes. They wore the pelts like big ragged capes, crudely cut and torn to make room for arms or legs. No gentle stitching with bone needles, like what made my tunics. No pounded leather in their footwear. A few bone, stone, or shell ornaments. Nothing like the fang on the necklace dangling over my chest. Even their weapons were worse. Spears, carved and fire-hardened—unlike mine, with a sharp flint point affixed by lines of sinew.

"What sort of Broadhead are they?" Autumn asked. "I am sorry, Red—I do not know much about Broadheads."

"I know them." I stood. "And the Hill Spirits are kind to us. They're Hillmen. The Hill Clan is good. If it was the Frost Clan, they would have attacked the encampment by now and killed all of us."

"I don't know if that's true..." Star said. "I would have fought them."

"You would have tried." I shrugged. "But it doesn't matter. I will go and talk to them."

I walked down from the hill and went to the edge of the Moon Pool, Good Wolf pawing along at my side. No point in hiding anymore. These were the Hill Clan. I knew them all. I held out both my hands and waved them. I screeched as loud as I could. The hunters stopped their conversation, faced me, and screeched back. Then I joined them.

They hugged me. They planted kisses on my cheeks. Their fingers played in the fine mammoth fur of my cloak and they whistled in amazement—and they stayed well-clear of Good Wolf, for fear of losing fingers. I just smiled and let it happen, as Star and Autumn hung back at the edge of the hazy light cast by the flame.

Rock, their leader, gave me the biggest hug of all. "Red." He took a step back. His hair and beard had gone gray, even though he was my age—and that had given him his name. "Red, it has been a long, long time. Many winters, many summers, and springs."

He spoke the language of the Hills. A stranger to my ears, but I still knew every word.

"I have missed you, Red. It is good to see you."

"How are you, Rock? How are the Children of the Hills?"

"Good, good, good." He smiled, brightening up suddenly. "I have a mate. You know him." He pointed to the edge of the fire. "Song! Look, it is Red."

"I can see that it is Red." Song approached. He linked his hands with Rock. Song was called Song because he sang everything. He sang his words now, adding little hums and twirls in each word. Some found it annoying, but Rock had always loved it—and him. "It has been a long time. Much, much time. We have all missed you." His singing slowed, and he tapped his feet against the gravel. "But you were not to be found. You were in the Heap."

"I am still in the Heap," I added.

That's when Star and Autumn approached. The other Hill Clan hunters did not like that. They hooted and screeched. Many brandished their spears or went for their clubs. Star's hand shot to the handle of her lance, and Autumn tensed up. Even if they didn't outnumber my friends, the Broadheads were bigger and stronger. Star might be a great warrior, but the Hill hunters would tear her apart.

"No!" I bellowed out the word—stomping my foot hard enough to raise dust. "Rock, Song—these ones walk with me. Our hearts beat together." Then I spoke to Star in the words of the Heap. "Do not pull the Lance of the Skies. Keep it on your back."

"Why not?" she demanded.

"If you draw it, you might use it—and these are my friends." The same words I had told the Broadheads, now said in the language of the Narrow Ones.

Star removed her fingers from the carved handle. She held up her hands— she trusted me.

Autumn gave the Broadheads her biggest smile. "Tell them that we won't bring harm. We are preparing to grow our plants here in the Fields, so we need the land. To plant the seeds and care for the plants, and to take to the fruits that grow. We could even trade with them. They just need to stay out of our way." She drew closer to me and gave me a hopeful smile. "Could you mention that, Red?"

I might as well try to teach Good Wolf how to paint a cave wall.

I faced Rock. "They do not want war."

Rock folded his arms. "Thin Noses like war. Eaters are Thin Noses—"

"These Thin Noses are not Eaters," Song suggested.

I nodded. "They aren't. They are from the Heap. The people of the Heap are good. There are many of them and some are bad, but most are good." I pointed to Autumn. "This is Autumn. She needs the dirt here. She wants to plant seeds, so that fruit will grow. When the fruit grows, there will be more food. She'll trade." I pointed to the hunters. "With you."

They stared at each other. A few made loud, insulting screeches. Rock pointed to Autumn. "She is stupid. But she can dig in the dirt, if she wants. We do not care. But we still need this land to hunt." He lowered his voice. "It is bad in the hills. There is less food. We are hungry in the hills."

"Thin Nose hunters kill so many," Song added. "Driving herds of mammoth off cliffs. Butchering ten or—or more than ten at a time. All for those good cloaks, like the one you wear." He made his song sad. "Less food for us."

"What are they talking about?" Autumn asked. "And why is that one singing?"

I faced her and switched to the speech of the Heap. "He is Song. Singing is what he does. But they have wrapped flowers around their words. They wish to be kind." That wasn't entirely true, but I saw no reason not to lie a little. "They won't bother you, as long as you do not bother them. So there is no need for war."

"Do they know that?" Star asked.

I looked back at Rock, Song, and the others. "You do not want war." I told them, rather than asked them. "Do you want war?"

"*We* don't," Rock said. "But the Frost Clan does."

The Frost People. They loved war. When I grew up in the hills, we would often fight with them. Twice as much as we fought with the Eaters or the other Thin Ones—for fighting is what the Frost Clan loved to do. Even their hunts were like war. They would rather come south from their cold mountains, kill the Broadheads of our tribe, and take what we had then find their own.

Still, there were times when we were at peace with them. We would trade and visit their camps and sing together. They could be as friendly as the Hill Clan, in the right circumstances. I had even played with the young of the Frost People, when I was small.

But my father never forgot the five notches on his club, that had been five Frost People warriors whose skulls he had split. Or the many friends that the Frost Clan had sent to dance with the Hill Spirits, who were now notches on their warriors' clubs.

But it didn't make sense. "The Frost Clan are north of here. In the mountains."

"They are coming south," Rock explained. "White Hair is bringing them south. Bad hunts. No food. Just like we have." White Hair—their headwoman. I heard stories about her. It was said she had wrestled a saber-tooth, and wrenched out its fangs with her bare hands—which she now wore, along with the tiger's white pelt. Rock shuddered. "They're coming south."

"Have you made war with the Frost Clan?"

"Not yet," Song said. "We live together. We hunt and trade together. But White Hair wants to come here. And she will not want peace."

It was a true problem, enough to put ice in my heart. If White Hair came with the Frost Clan and the Hill Clan, and put them together, and took them to war, then that war would be very bad. The Heap had many good warriors, who had practiced in fighting the Eaters. But Broadheads were stronger, and their desperation would give them strength. They might win, and tear the Heap apart in search of food, crushing all the strange inventions that the Narrow Faces had made under their feet.

Many would die, no matter who won.

I looked back at Star and Autumn. They must have known how bad the news was.

"The Frost Clan's coming here," I said. "Driven south by hunger. They're seeking friendship with the Hills. Together, they'll take the Flowering Fields."

"We need the Flowering Fields," Autumn said. "We need it to grow."

Star bit her lip and looked at the sky. The sun had set for good now—the Night Demons bearing it down until the Spirits could bring it back up for the morning. Moonlight shone over the bluish grass, turning everything gray before it went black. It added a brilliant shine to the Moon Pools in front of us.

Night—the time of Night Demons and danger. We needed to go back.

Star had folded her hands. Praying to those Southern Gods, perhaps? "This is bigger than us." She pointed to Rock. "You tell him to come to the Heap. Bring the leader of the Frost People with him. What's she called?"

"White Hair," I replied.

"Are your names all based on colors, or objects, or sounds?" Autumn asked.

Star winked at her. "And you, named for a season." She faced me. "Whatever she's called—tell your friends to invite her to the Heap. The Tooth King can talk it over. Create peace." Star motioned to Autumn. "She can plant her seeds, and the Broadheads can hunt. Everyone's happy. How's that sound?"

"I'll ask." I faced Rock and Song, who had been watching the dancing fire. Growing bored. "I make a request to you: send a message to White Hair. The Tooth King wants to meet with her, and you."

"But what will he do in this meeting?" Song asked, in his singsong way.

"He will talk with you. Make—" I struggled to find the Broadhead word. "An agreement. Make peace, between you and White Hair and him."

"White Hair does not like to make peace," Rock said. "She likes war."

"She might like the peace the Tooth King will give her," I said. "Otherwise, the ravens will eat all our bones."

Rock's smile fell away. "If there was a war between the People and the Heap, Red, which side would you fight for?"

It was a cruel question. "That is a cruel question!" I told him, raising my voice until it went shrill.

Song glared at Rock. "It was. We know you would choose us."

I said nothing more on the subject. If I did, then might think worse of me. Besides, there wouldn't be war between the Heap and the Broadheads. The Tooth King was smart. He would make sense of things. "So, you will tell White Hair?"

"We will tell White Hair," Rock agreed. "Now, will you stay by the fire? Song will sing. We will roast the meat we killed during the day and tell stories."

That was how most nights ended in the hills. I considered it. Seated by the fire, laughing at the funny stories that we would take turns telling. Huddling together under the skins—and then the morning, waking up cold and stiff and hating our bones while we tried to cook something to quiet the rumbling in our bellies. It probably wouldn't taste very good. Not compared to the breakfasts that Narrow Ones made.

"I have to go with them." I pointed to Star and Autumn. "I'm sorry. But I'll see you, when you come to the Heap."

"Yes." Rock offered his hand. "I will see you when I come to the Heap."

We clasped hands and embraced a final time, and then I turned away. I rejoined Autumn, who had busied herself with petting Good Wolf. Star folded her arms, clearly impatient. "Well?"

"They've agreed. They'll tell White Hair, and Rock will come to the Heap to speak for the Hills. We'll figure something out."

Autumn smiled. "Ah—a good ending. Like all the best stories." The moonlight added a shine to her pale face. The freckles stood out like berries in the snow. I watched her for a moment, scratching the fur behind Good Wolf's ear, before she stood up. "Well, it is nearly full dark. The stars are bright, at least. They'll guide our way back." She paused. "Unless you want to stay here, Red. With the other Broadheads."

I looked back and knew that I did not.

"We'll lead you back."

Star moved ahead, stepping over the grass. We stared back through the deer trail, past the grazing aurochs—back to the people of the Heap.

They were my people now. I still spoke the language of the Broadheads. I still knew their songs. But I would never go back to the hills. Even before I knew I didn't have the strength to survive out there, I did not belong amongst those cold stones. In the Heap, you could survive by talking, by helping people, and—occasionally—by hurting. Being a Fang was what I was good at. Not being a Broadhead.

Still, I looked over my shoulder as we loped back through the tall grass. Good Wolf seemed to sense my disappointment. She went to my side and rubbed against my legs, whining as her ears flicked back. Or maybe she just wanted more pets.

I petted her and we went back.

Everyone prepared their furs for the night. Gummy had appointed a few sentries, to stand at the far ends and watch the Fields for Eaters. Then, he had gone to sleep—not staying awake to fulfill his end of the bargain. Nearly hairless, and curled up in a bear fur blanket beside the fire, his chewing slaves slumbering next to him, he looked like an oversized infant bundled up by his mother.

Star looked at him and then to Raven, who sat on the log by the firepit with his obsidian-edged club on his lap. "Are you going to wake him?" Raven asked.

"I'm thinking about it."

He sucked his teeth. "Don't. Wait until morning."

"Don't put fire in your words. We'll be here." She pointed to a path of grass a bit away from the main camp. "Red, we'll slumber there. At least we don't have to worry about taking watches."

Autumn went to her own bedroll, an intricately-stitched blanket of striped cave hyena pelts. She glanced back at me. "It was good to meet you." She smiled suddenly. "We'll have fruit tomorrow. For breakfast. Grown from some of the trees by the riverside. Not grown by my hands. Not yet."

"I will be hungry in the morning." I waved back to her and followed Star.

She had a satchel containing deer skins and bundled cushions, which she laid down—along with chunks of spiced jerky and roots for dinner. We ate hungrily, and I tossed the leftovers to Good Wolf. We washed it all down with fresh river water, wrapped ourselves in our mammoth cloaks, and lay down.

Star mimicked Autumn's words in a singsong voice. "We'll have fruit tomorrow..." She faced the sky with her hands folded behind her head.

"Why are you saying that?" I glared at her. "Pretending to be Autumn."

"Just putting myself in her mind. I think she really wants to feed you, Red. She'll serve you a whole dinner, with a smile on her face."

"What?" I squinted. "She's being kind to a guest. Even the Narrow Face gods teach that. You must be kind to the stranger."

"She doesn't want you to stay a stranger, Red."

"No!" I rolled over, refusing to face Star. "You don't know what you're talking about."

"You are blinding your own eyes. Even Broadheads aren't *that* stupid."

I grabbed a handful of dirt and chucked it at her. The clod settled on her blanket and made Good Wolf sit up and bark. Star brushed it off and glared back. "I think it's nice. You've been alone in your cave for too long."

"And what about you?"

"What about me?"

"Do you have somebody? I've seen different men and women in your cave, but they never stay for long…"

This time, she sent dirt whistling at me. "Go to sleep, Red."

I rolled over and went to sleep.

That night, the Hill Spirits sent me a dream. Or maybe it was the Night Demons, because the dream wasn't very good. Whoever it was, they plucked me out of the Flowering Field and carried me far away, to some frozen mountains. Probably to the north. This was the place where the Hill People would send hunting parties, especially when winter came and beasts could not be found. We would seek the big, furry animals. Mammoths or oxen or rhinos. Always a difficult hunt; but if it worked, we'd return with frozen meat and bones and ivory and all would celebrate.

This time, I wandered up a slope alone, bundled in patchwork fur and carrying a Broadhead spear. My father walked ahead of me, bearing a torch. Dead for many seasons, and yet there he was. He was hunched over, his head half-hidden behind his shoulders. His beard and hair, red, like mine, mingled with his furs, so he seemed to be one furry creature, like the mammoth or the rhino.

"Father!" I called out to him, but he kept walking. Trudging ahead into the cold.

The wind blew. It sliced at my skin and stirred up the snow. The white flurries danced around me, washing over the mountain. Warning that the cold was coming, and the starving and war would come with it.

Maybe even the Heap couldn't hold it back.

I tried to run. I slipped in the snow. My father walked on and vanished in the cold.

My eyes flickered open and I slipped out of the Night Demons' grip. Good Wolf darted to me a moment later, yipping and excited—her tail jabbing upward. She pawed at me, delivering little, excited punches to my belly and face. I rolled over and sat up. Calmed her with a few pets. She pointed her nose into the distance.

She'd smelled something the sentries hadn't seen.

Eaters? She'd be barking if that was the case.

I grabbed my spear and patted her back. Good Wolf walked down to the riverbank, away from Star. Should I wake her? No—let her rest a little more. If there really was danger, I would shout very loudly. Besides, I wouldn't go that far. Instead, I followed Good Wolf down along the river.

We went a few paces away from the camp. Then Good Wolf stopped, going low on her belly. The hunter's way. I crouched low and looked ahead.

There, on the other side of the river. Giant shapes, outlines in the darkness. Mammoths. They loomed tall, half-hidden in shadow. Moonlight glimmered on the tusks, making them shine like polished bone. A small herd, maybe ten or fifteen mammoths strong. They lined up together, standing together and letting their trunks slip into the river. The calves moved up next, darting past their mothers and the young bulls to play in the shallows. A few trumpets sounded, and some sent spurts of water into the air, which fell with a splash back into the river.

I had seen mammoths before, but the sight always took the breath from my mouth. The size of them, the power in their legs—it was like watching the mountains move.

Some Broadheads said that the Hill Spirits worked hard on mammoths, and spent days getting the form just right. Thin Noses had the Elephant Mother, the mammoth goddess who watched kindly over her children.

They were both right, as far as I thought. There had to be something magical about creatures this magnificent.

Good Wolf perked up. Feet crunched in the grass. I spun around, gripping my spear. It was only Autumn. She settled on her knees next to me and we looked back at the mammoths together.

"By the Gods." She whispered the word. "Look at them! Do you see the way they work together?" She seemed as excited as a child recounting a storyteller's favorite works.

"They must. One mammoth alone is vulnerable. Prey for a wolf pack or a cave lion or a tiger. But together? Nothing can stop them."

"True enough, Red. But there are rules they follow. The big one—she is their queen. And those at the sides. They're sentries. Using their tusks like fences. After them, you see the mothers? The cows? They're bathing each other. Shooting water into their fur. And all of them watch the calves."

It was all true. I wouldn't think of anything like that.

"Do they talk to each other? How to know who should go where?"

"I don't know. Some animals are alone. Tigers, for instance. Or cave bears. A mother is with her cubs, and that's it. The fathers don't stay with them—or are even a threat. But other creatures, like those mammoths, and your dog there—or her father, who was a wolf—need to be with their kind. They have to work together."

"By the gods. Look at them!"

"What about Narrow Faces and Broadheads?"

"Narrow Faces and Broadheads too." Autumn grinned at me. "The Gods made us to stay together."

For a while, we stared at each other. The mammoths trumpeted and spurted water. Their calves played. I felt a fire in my heart—but not of anger or sadness. I wanted Autumn closer to me.

Then Good Wolf let out a sudden bark. I turned away—the warm fire switching to a burning fear. Was there danger? I stood and gripped my spear. Good Wolf looked into the woods, across the stream. Her ears had flicked back. She'd smelled something more than the mammoths, more than the usual animals that made their homes in the woods. But what?

I had to see.

"Red?" Autumn asked.

I stood. "I think—I think there's something in the woods. Eaters, maybe."

"Oh—Gods!" Her mouth opened.

"Go back to the camp. Stay with Star. Or Raven. I'll see what it is and deal with it. Or come back and get more help."

"You're certain? It could be dangerous. If it's a cave lion or a tiger—"

I offered her my hand—bigger than hers. "I'll be careful."

She clasped it for a moment and then stood up and hurried back. Keeping low and crawling her away through the grass, so she wouldn't be spotted. A very smart Narrow One woman. Then I rested my spear on my shoulder and started through the grass, Good Wolf pawing along next to me.

We reached the river—a shallower band of fast-flowing water, with pale stones beneath. I crossed, Good Wolf loping a little ahead. Downstream, the mammoths snorted and a few trumpeted. The big mother, her eyes dark and glowering, shifted around and watched us between her tusks. I made no move to attack and neither did she.

Then we reached the other side.

Good Wolf had gone quiet. Wolves could be quiet. Every creature in the forest knew that. She walked carefully amongst the trees, nose twitching as she led me along. I drifted after her, taking care to match her silence. My eyes had adjusted to the lowlight. I could see a little—but not much. So going slow, not walking into a branch was best.

Then Good Wolf stopped. She sniffed up ahead.

Fire shone in the darkness—bright as a fallen star. There, in a tall tree near the water's edge. Someone sat there, a torch set in a forked branch above them to provide flickering light. A man's shape. Too small for a Broadhead. A Thin Nose. Crouched up there, like a leopard waiting for prey to pass under so it could pounce.

Had they noticed me? I slid behind the bole of a tall tree and patted Good Wolf's back. She lay down in the undergrowth. We stayed still as the moment passed. The splashes, trumpeting, and shuffling of the mammoth herd came in the distance. Was it an Eater up there? Probably not. They always traveled in groups. The better to haul back prisoners for eating.

I peered out for a better look.

A dark figure, wearing a cloak made from black cave lion's skin. A hooded form. He sat there for a moment, watching the mammoths, and then turned—and looked in my direction. I slid back behind the tree. Trying to hide.

But I caught a glimpse of him in the moonlight. It shone on his face—or his mask. A mask of bone, made from the skull of a great ape.

I had seen this Night Demon before. The mushroom that Mother Rat gave me showed me—and now, there he was. The one who had plunged his knife into Frog Face and filled his mouth with dirt.

The Blood-Spiller.

I peered out again. Good Wolf had stood up—agitated. The Blood-Spiller reached to his back, where a quiver waited. He pulled an arrow free as he took a short bow from his cloak. Hard to see in the dark, but it looked like a good weapon, made of polished, carved wood and antler, with a fine gut string. It would cost many teeth.

He set the arrow in the torch until the head burned, and put the shaft to his bowstring.

He was going to loose it at the Flowering Fields. Would it start a fire? Burn the grass? Catch Star, Autumn, and the others in the blaze? I couldn't let him.

I left my hiding place. I ran for the Night Demon, screeching a Broadhead war cry as I hoisted my spear. Good Wolf ran with me, letting out a long and powerful howl.

The Blood-Spiller spun about. His face faced mine. I caught a glimpse of his eyes—a shade of light blue—and then he pulled back the bowstring and set the arrow whistling in my direction. It descended like a comet, trailing smoke and fire.

I threw myself to the ground. Only that saved me. The arrow thudded into the dirt behind me. It startled Good Wolf, who ran out of the way with a set of yips—vanishing amongst the trees. I pulled myself and looked back at the Blood-Spiller. If I could reach him, I could pull him down—and then I'd put all my Broadhead strength to work. Break his bones. Or just drive the spear straight through him, and leave it there.

He had another arrow at the string—not on fire at least. I ducked behind a tree. It whistled down and stabbed into the wood next to me. Quivering slightly before staying in place. I gripped my spear tightly. How many arrows did he have? A third shaft didn't come flying in my direction.

But the string twanged. The arrow sailed away. Not at me, though. What was he doing?

Then I heard the trumpets. I peered out. He'd sent another fiery arrow—straight in the direction of the mammoths. The arrow arced up and settled amongst them. He'd aimed it right. The arrow didn't hit a mammoth, but settled into the grass at their feet. Fires licked at the grass on the riverbank. Not enough to start a true blaze.

But enough to panic the mammoths.

A big cow was the first to notice. She twisted around, trumpeted loudly, and started to run. The smaller males and the mothers joined in as well, forming a ring around the calves as the fire danced along the grass at their feet.

They came charging into the woods. Straight at me.

I glanced away from the stampede and back at the Blood-Spiller.

He had vanished.

CHAPTER THREE
WINTER'S BARRED FANGS

The whole earth trembled, like the Hill Spirits were roaring and raging just under the dirt. The fire growing in the grass beyond sent crazy shadows dancing through the cold moonlight as the massive forms of the mammoths started to move.

Hard to make out the individual beasts as they came crashing toward the forest, breaking branches with their tusks or shoving smaller trees aside with their bulk. They came as one stampeding mass. Making the earth rumble and leaves fall from the trees and come whirling down in a wild rain. Fire danced behind them, and their eyes caught the glimmer of the moonlight as their trumpeting echoed through the Bloodwood and the riverbanks.

Like the Blood-Spiller could rend the world apart, and command the fire and the beasts whenever he wanted.

He was a Night Demon. I was certain.

I had to get out of the way. I had to find Good Wolf. Where was that dog?

My eyes flecked over the forest. I forced the sounds apart. The trumpeting, the crashing, the beating of my heart with the knowledge that I would be crushed or trampled in a moment. I heard it—Good Wolf's yipping and barking. I spun around. There she was, back arched and tail raised, ears tented. Letting out bark after bark. As terrified as I was.

I reached her in one step. Grabbed the scruff of her neck as I took hold of a low hanging branch. Good Wolf was a heavy dog. But I had big arms, full of Broadhead strength. I pushed her up. She fought me, jabbing with her claws and barking and shaking—until I had her on the branch. She'd jump off a moment later and fall down. Into the path of the mammoths.

I couldn't let that happen.

They were close nose. Smashing their way through the trees. Coming toward me. A young mammoth emerged out of the shadows and fire. The tusks curled upward, brilliant white—moonlight made smooth and sharp. Leaves clung to the thick fur, and its eyes flashed with panic.

Had to get into the trees. Away from those pounding feet. I grabbed the bough above of me and pressed my feet against the tree's bole. My good spear dangled on its strap, jabbing into my back as I grabbed and pulled. Got one arm up, and then my shoulder and my leg. The trumpeting came closer. I went up, next to Good Wolf. She barked at me and tried to jump down. I grabbed her and held tight.

The mammoth charged into the clearing. One tusk and a shoulder slammed into the tree. It shook. Leaves rained down. Smaller branches broke. The mammoth's side rushed by. Close enough for a hint of the fur to scratch my arm.

This time, Good Wolf realized what jumping down would mean. She pressed against me and howled.

The other mammoths followed. Smaller trees went down, but the Hill Spirits were good to me. They held my tree up. It did not fall and I did not go under the mammoth feet and meet my Wrong Death. Instead, it shook and banged my legs and back against the trunk to raise welts while Good Wolf's paws jabbed against me.

But we didn't fall.

The mammoths charged on and on for what seemed to be a winter and a summer and half of fall as well. Then, the calves ran under our feet—too weak to do much damage. They hurried off into the shadows, still smashing trees and shaking the earth.

Then they were gone and the forest exhaled.

A flock of birds had left their nighttime perches further out in the woods. They fluttered up in a squawking, calling mass that danced and shifted before vanishing into the night sky. A cave lion roared, and a panther of some sort took up the call with a shriek. Other animals voiced their fears as the mammoth herd stampede thundered away.

I look at Good Wolf. Her tongue had jabbed out, bright pink and quivering. She panted, her whole body shaking. I embraced her and she licked my face furiously. We slipped down from the branch and settled back onto the dirt.

The world still spun. I sat down until it stopped spinning. Glanced back at the branches above us. No—no sign of the Blood-Spiller. He had fired his arrow, sent mammoths to trample me, and gone.

What was I doing here? The Broadheads of my people, the Hill People, had greeted me with happy calls. Rock and Song accepted me like I had never left. Like I had woke in the cave on another bright day, ready to hunt or dig up roots alongside them. But I wasn't with them. I was with the Narrow Faces, and I had been nearly crushed by mammoths thanks to a Night Demon that they had summoned.

I rested the spear in the earth and used it like a staff. Helped myself up and got some strength back into my legs. Good Wolf swirled around me, tail still shaking. I scratched her behind the ears as I slung the spear back over my back and started for the river.

Autumn. I had to see her.

Out of the trees and back to the creek. Snowmelt water played over my toes. It felt nice. I went back to the camp, past the makeshift stockade. Now, torches flashed amongst Gummy's gatherers. They clustered together, many reaching for bows or clutching their spears or axes. Nothing like a mammoth stampede to wake people up.

Hard to see amongst the firelight and darkness. I had sent Autumn back to join them. Had she made it? Was she safe? It put ice in my heart, not knowing—but why? I had just met her a few hours ago.

But she was alive—and life had to be preserved.

"That's far enough!" A call from a dark shape near a hillock overlooking the creek. I hadn't seen Raven. But I saw him now. He had that obsidian-edged club raised in one hand, the moon making the dark stone extra shiny. His other hand contained a strange device—a pair of round stones connected by a slim cord. He spun them around and around, fast enough to make them hum. Would he send them spinning at my head? His face remained shrouded in darkness. I couldn't tell.

I stopped and shifted my shoulder. The spear fell into my hand. Next to me, Good Wolf arched her back and let out a low growl. Neither of us were in the mood.

"Stop! Stay still, Broadhead!" Raven shouted the command. "Not one step further."

Star appeared next to him. "Throw it and I'll put this through your back." The Lance of the Skies rested in her hands. "Red's no enemy."

"He's not like us." But Raven did slacken his arm. The ropes and stones went slack. "Where I come from, there are none like him. And the ones who are here, in the fields, threatened Gummy's gatherers. Now this one wanders off at night, and mammoths charge, and fires burn—and then he comes back." His dark eyes matched the raven feathers in his cape. "You can put a fang necklace around him. It doesn't make him like us."

"Take the fire away from your words when you speak of Red." Star spoke calmly—but the rage was there, just under the surface. "Or he won't be the one you have to worry about."

Sticking up for me—pride surged in my heart.

"No—please—I was with him!" Autumn's voice.

I whispered a prayer of thanks to the Hill Spirits.

She emerged from the edge of the camp, next to Gummy. Autumn's face bore lines of worry. "Gummy—he protected me. He sent me back here."

Raven looked at Gummy. The old man nodded. That did the job. Raven let those spinning orbs go still and returned it to the pouch under his cape. Then he folded his arms behind his back, and went silent. Gummy beckoned me over and I went. Out of the river and over the grass. Behind us, the blaze in the field near the riverbank had started to fade. Not much fuel for it to take, there in the patchwork grass close to the river. Lines of smoke still drifted up, making the dark sky gray.

We went back to the camp. Gummy's slave children had already started chewing up some vegetables and fruits, bowls clasped in their hands. Gummy patted the shoulder of the boy as he slumped down on a log and motioned us to sit in front of him. Like the children gathering before the elder, ready to hear a story.

Except I'd be telling the story this time.

"The Blood-Spiller." I settled down, the fire to my back. Good Wolf curled up next to me and rested her head on my knee. "I found him in the Bloodwood."

"Who is the Blood-Spiller?" Gummy asked.

"The one who gave Frog Face the Wrong Death." Star shrugged. "He spilled blood. Red called him the Blood-Spiller. I suppose the name's fitting."

"Fair enough." Gummy bobbed his head. "How do you know it was him?"

"The same mask—the mask of a skull of a giant ape. A cloak as dark as midnight. Mother Rat told me that the one who bought the stolen seed—the one in Frog Face's mouth—wore the skull of a giant ape as a mask." I stared at my knuckles. "He watched us from the trees. Watching the camp. When I chased him, he sent an arrow wrapped in fire into the mammoths. Must've hoped that they would crush me."

"Thank the Elephant Mother that they did not," Autumn said.

"And where did he go?" Gummy asked. "Did you chase him?"

That was what Fangs were supposed to do. When someone broke the Tooth

King's laws, we hunted them down like wolves hunting prey. But I had been the prey and the Blood-Spiller had vanished. "No. He ran into the Bloodwood. He might be out there now."

Silence followed my words. There was only the slave children's chewing and the crackling of fire. The youngsters spat together into the bowl. The girl held her bowl, offering it to Gummy. His face had changed. The wrinkles deepened and he cupped his hairless chin and stroke the stubble. The young slave pushed the bowl closer, holding her breath.

He smashed it out of her hand. Fruit pulp and spittle rained onto the soil. Gummy sprang to his feet, moving faster than old bones should allow. "We'll leave the Fields. Start taking what we can. We'll move west, back into the forest. Closer to the Heap."

Autumn stood as well. "Gummy, we cannot. There are more seeds to be collected. I have to plant more, to see what can grow as it get colder. If sunlight is enough or if there needs to be warmth. The forest is no place to grow the—"

"If you want my help, and my teeth to pay for the protection of your seeds and your planting, you'll do as you're told." He snarled at her—toothlessly, but Autumn still flinched. "We leave as soon as we can pack our supplies. Accept it or go back to scrounging."

She said nothing. Gummy walked off, his two slave children and Raven falling in step behind him. All around us, Gummy's gatherers went to work folding up bedrolls, loading up baskets, and packing what they could. It was still dark and they were still tired. Fatigue clung to them, and made them slow, but they didn't argue or protest.

Autumn looked at me and said nothing—then she went to the riverside to gather her seeds.

Star and I stayed by the dying fire. She used the butt of her lance to push over a fallen log, sending up a rush of sparks. They floated up, past her face. She bit her lip and her eyes flicked back and forth. I knew that look.

"What are you thinking?"

"Gummy's terrified."

"Who wouldn't he be scared of the Blood-Spiller?"

"No." She shook her head. "It's more than that, Red. Everyone's scared of the Blood-Spiller. But Gummy fears that he'll be next. The question is—why?"

I didn't know. I also didn't want to ask.

We reached the Heap the next day, a little after dawn. Morning came later and later as the night grew long and the air went cold. Frost hung in the air. The Hill Spirits would bring the snow soon, and animals would grow thin or run south where the Heap's hunters couldn't follow. In the hills, winter brought death and starvation. It wasn't the same here. Star had told me that yesterday—but the fear remained.

Fear of Eaters too, though we didn't encounter any. We were ready, Good Wolf sniffing around and Star clutching the handle of her lance at every bark. Turned out to be squirrels and monkeys. The Eater she had killed said that he was beloved of Big Mouth—that eating human flesh let Big Mouth see everything, and he would know and come for her. But if she was scared, she didn't show it.

Winter and Eaters at our back. The Night Demons' tongues lolling, dripping with hunger at the prospect of rending our flesh.

Then the Heap, looming out of the morning mist. Shimmering with more lights—torchlight, firelight—than I could count. Cooking smells of roasting meat and vegetables drifting out of the caves and wafting down. Traders started to call out their wares, and a band played somewhere—a chorus of flutes followed by cheerful drumming. A place of warmth and people.

It was good to be back.

We passed the fisherwoman huts and hunter huts sprawling out from the length of the mountain, and took the slope leading up. "The Tooth King?" I asked Star.

"The Tooth King," she agreed. "To tell him of what happened, and about the Frost Clan and the Hill Clan. If anyone can stop a war, it's him." We passed a frog pond, its owner using a stick to break the ice crusting on the surface. "You want a frog? I'm buying."

"Why not?" It would be a nice break after the breakfast of deer jerky, dried berries, and cold water that we'd gobbled down while on the move. "I am hungry enough to eat ten frogs and then eat ten more frogs."

Broadhead bellies always needed filling.

Star grinned and held out three fingers to the Pond Man as she fished a single tooth from the pouch on her belt. He had some frogs already roasting on skewers over some hot coals, and he tossed some herbs over them before handing them over, wrapped in scraps of skin for the grease.

We sat down on some flat stones near the pond and gnawed on the frogs. The flesh had the right chew in it, and the spice put a good fire in my tongue. Then Star glanced down the trail and groaned. "Holy Desert Winds, I beg of you—carry me away, so I don't have to deal with *her*."

Spinner walked up the trail and stood across from us. She had chestnut-colored hair shorn short and a huge smile, a pair of shining stone piercings worked into her nose and ears. "Our two heroic Fangs, returned from battling the demons." She folded her arms as she leaned closer. "Eating a well-deserved victory meal."

I took a large bite of frog and chewed loudly. "Let it be a victory meal that is undisturbed by you, Tale-Spinner."

"No need to put fire in your words, lovely Red." Spinner drew closer to us. "Just talk to me about what you encountered. I need a little more spice to my tales for the firesides. How else am I to earn the teeth that feed me? You don't want me to starve, do you?" She wore a fine tunic and cloak of stitched otter fur, mingled with the softy pelts of sloths—she was in no danger of starving.

"Come on, Red." Star patted my arm and we stood up. "We'll eat and walk." She glared at Spinner. "You'll survive without learning details. You'll just make something up. That's what you do anyway."

We started up the slope, Good Wolf padding along beside us.

But Spinner stayed close behind. "Please, Star. Will you make me beg?"

She spun around and glared at Spinner. She would probably follow us all day, bothering us until we told her. "Put this in your stories—we seek a Blood-Spiller, a man who spills blood without reason, who gives the Wrong Death to good people. He wears a mask made from an ape's skull because he's afraid to show his face. But I'll see it—and then I'll give him the death he's earned. If anyone has seen someone with an ape's skull, tell a Fang. We'll find him."

"He might be a Night Demon," I added.

"He's not a Night Demon," Star corrected. "Is that enough for you, Tale-Spinner? Then don't linger."

She gave a good child's hopeful smile. "That's not what you said a few nights ago."

Star made an exasperated noise and turned around, her mammoth fur cloak spinning. I trailed after her, Good Wolf at my heels. Spinner ran off—probably to start practicing her story for the fires that night. It might even help us catch the Blood-Spiller, and at least it got Spinner off our backs.

I wasn't sure what she had meant about Star wanting her to linger.

We neared another level of the mountain, where my cave waited. "Red!" Mouse called to me. She sat on a ledge with a few orphans. They had been spitting at the heads of people going up and down the hill. Already, the boy next to her had snorted in his snot, getting ready to spit. Mouse slapped the back of his head and made his spittle fall on his bare feet, then scrambled over the ledge and dropped down to join us.

She hurried over and gave Good Wolf a hug, in return for several sloppy licks. "How are you, Mouse?" Star asked.

"Oh, well enough." Mouse looked up at me and Star. "Have fun in the Bloodwood?"

"We were nearly eaten by cannibals and trampled by mammoths." I snapped my fingers and pointed to her. Good Wolf patted over. "Can you look after her for the day? We are going to see the Tooth King. It's best that she stays here."

"It would put sunlight around my heart," Mouse agreed.

"And I have something for you." I reached into my pouch and drew it out—a flower from the Flowering Fields. The petals had been crushed a little in the journey, but they still had the color. I held it out. Mouse accepted it carefully. She rolled the flower around in her fingers, feeling the smoothness of the petals, before tucking it behind her ear. "You like it?" I asked.

She beamed. "I'm the Tooth Queen of the Heap."

I let her take Good Wolf back to my cave. Spinner calling me a hero—even though there was a bit of humor in it—and Mouse being glad to see me—those were good things. And Star had stood up for me, back in the Fields. It meant that some in the Heap cared for me, and that I had friends there. Just as much as in the Hills.

For whatever that was worth.

We kept going. Up the slope, past the Cave of the Gods and all the idols and altars. Further up. Under ladders and bridges of wood and stone, draped with flowers. Another walk around the length of the Heap, up the switchback trails, and we neared the peak. Here, dwellings of stone and wood rested behind arches of intricately carved mammoth tusks. Slaves carried about litters of the richest Thin Noses—the ones with bags of teeth hidden in their caves. They had elegant embroidery on their robes and tunics. Shining stones worked into their staffs and scepters. Dyes in their hair. Slaves to carry their extra garments, cook their food, and take the hands of their children.

Fangs rarely went here. I had only been twice. It was like I had taken a wrong turn and entered the world of the Hill Spirits, where they drank gold and swam in sunlight.

Star patted my shoulder. "Don't be frightened. They might be rich, but they're still flesh and blood."

"You know that for certain?"

"I grew up around people like this." She grimaced. "Trust me—they're not special."

We went further up and neared the peak. The mountain top loomed above, with the best cave of all inside. The first one settled, which made the whole Heap. The Cave of the Tooth King. A tent of sable furs with supports of carved tusks and antlers formed a long tunnel, leading inside. Star pulled back the tent flap and we entered.

Scented fire drifted up. A few of the Tooth King's court lounged on cushions or blankets, drinking fermented fruit juice while slaves tended to them. A musician in the corner worked a rattle made from a tortoise shell—but he froze up when we entered. The others did too. Like ice had fallen over all of them.

They weren't used to seeing a Broadhead Fang.

"We need to see the king." Star kept her tone even. "He's further back, in his cave?"

"Did he ask you to come here?" Purple Plume—commander of the Feathers. The Tooth King's best. He walked over from the back of the tent, a pair of other Feathers flanking him. Fangs and Feathers didn't get along. Plume had his hair cut short, his beard shaved to stubble, and had—true to his name—purple plumes worked into his broad-brimmed straw hat and the shoulders of his cape. "I don't recall him asking for you."

"You might have forgotten," Star said. "Too busy cleaning your pretty plumes."

That was supposed to be a joke. I didn't get it, but I made a show of laughing loudly anyway.

Purple Plume's eyes went to me. "And you bring *that* with you." He walked closer, his spear—also with purple plumes around the point—held at an angle. "If the Tooth King wants his pet Broadhead to come, he'll call for him. The same with any dog."

Cruel words, meant to hurt. To make me angry. They succeeded. I snorted loudly, and my voice came out shrill. "You're wrong. I'm not a dog. Dogs have fur!"

Plume shook his head and turned his spear out—putting the point at Star. "Take him back down the mountain. I'll talk to the King. If he wants, we'll send for you. Otherwise, let the big fool—"

Star glared at the spear. "Point that spear elsewhere and we'll talk."

An ornate spearhead, aimed at my friend. It put fire in my heart just to think of it. My fingers grew tense, my muscles readying. Who did this little, weak-boned Thin Nose think he was? He might as well wrestle a mammoth as anger me—and he shouldn't threaten my friend.

He hesitated, his eyes widening—maybe revealing that he had made a mistake. Then he repeated his command. "Walk out of the cave and—"

"You will not point a spear at her!" I roared out the words and grabbed the spear.

My hand settled around the shaft, just below the spray of feathers. They tickled my fingers as I wrenched the spear closer. Purple Plume managed to keep hold of the spear, though his feet dragged on the stone floor. I punched him. That made him let go. Then I punched him again, a powerful, wild blow right into the tip of his chin. He flew back, jewelry clattering as he crashed hard to the ground.

The other Feathers hurried to help. A lean Feather with a necklace of flowers and a face stained with freckles, jabbed his spear out—trying to skewer me. Star's Lance of the Skies sliced down first. Crashing against his spear, nearly cutting into the wood, and forcing it down. "Red—stop this!" She called to me. "You're not helping!"

I grabbed the Feather by his floral necklace and tugged—dragging him right into my fist. He went back, arms spinning in the air. "How am I not helping?" The Feather dropped onto a pair of seated courtiers, spilling their fruit juice and sending them scrambling back in terror.

"Enough!" The roar came from past the tent. The mouth of a cave covered in colorful paintings. The Tooth King's voice, emanating from his home. "The fight will end!"

Everyone froze. It was like the Hill Spirits had spoken.

I pointed to Plume, now standing up and coughing. "They started it."

"Red, Star—is that you?"

Star removed her hat and bowed her head. "It is, O Tooth King. Glory to the Tooth King." She added those last words in a nervous afterthought.

"Come to my cave and speak with me." The King paused. "Plume? Clean up the mess. And stay there."

"They came here without thought, Tooth King!" Plume cried. "Dragging their stinking carcasses—"

"If I wanted to hear your tongue, I'd have it cut out and slap it against the walls of my cave." Another exasperated sigh. "Red, Star—you've already interrupted enough of my bath time. Come here and tell me what you want to say."

I exchanged a glance with Star. You didn't turn down an invitation from the Tooth King. She patted my shoulder as I rubbed my knuckles—a little sore after the punches. We stepped over the fallen Feather and the stunned courtiers, and walked our way into the cave.

Past the stone entrance, with torches set in the wall and providing light. Gaps in the ceiling had been widened, allowing more light to filter in. Every inch of stone had been covered in paintings. No pictures of the gods here. Only the Tooth King, standing tall and holding up a shimmering, giant tooth above his head—his realization of the miracle of what teeth could be. Another showing all the people of the Heap and the beasts of the land bowing to him. Others just showed teeth, running up and down in rows. They had been painted green or red or blue—colors that teeth shouldn't be. More Narrow Face foolishness.

Though I had to admit, they were pretty.

He had numerous animals too. Pets—that was the word for it. Like I had Good Wolf. Except that the Tooth King had a pair of cave hyenas in the pen in the corner, both curled up and sleeping now, next to a set of bones for them to gnaw on. Colorful birds sat in cages dangling from the ceiling. A half-dozen slaves tended to all the various animals. He even had a few wildcats, about the size of monkeys, their speckled pelts shining in the low light, which pawed around in the corners or made mad leaps onto the fine furnishings.

One such cat approached me. I went still. Such creatures belonged in the trees. But the cat pressed against my leg. Good Wolf would do such things. I stuck out my hand—as if to push it away. Instead, the cat rubbed itself against my hand. The fur amazingly soft. It made deep purring noise, its tail going straight up—and then went on its way.

This was pure magic.

"Do you like them, Red?" The Tooth King's voice. He sat in a pool made from stone and drizzled with flower petals. "Cats to join the dogs we already have." Star and I walked closer. One slave poured in more water, heated in a clay jug over hot coals. Another drizzled in flowers and herbs. The King looked like a bathing mammoth without the fur. "Why, you might ask? Why do we need them?"

"The question did occur," Star said.

"Think of it. We'll have food—grown from the earth. More than we can eat. So we'll store it. Pots and sacks of good food. But then they'll come—the rats and the mice." He paddled his way to the edge of the bath and rested his head in his thick hands. "But if we have the cats, they can eat the mice first. And protect our food stores. That's what I do. I find something that can help the Heap, and I bring it here."

Was he talking about me?

He pointed to Star. "The one who killed Frog Face."

"The Blood-Spiller," I added.

"The Blood-Spiller." The Tooth King nodded. "You have a way with words, Red. Have you found him?"

I looked at my shoes. "No, O Tooth King. I came close. In the forests outside the Flowering Fields. He sent a herd of mammoths to trample me, and escaped. But we know that he wears a mask made from the skull of an ape and a dark cloak."

"And that he's after Gummy," Star said. "Gummy fears him. He said someone else should fear the Blood-Spiller too. Who worked with Gummy, and Frog Face. And you."

"Scribbles the scribe. Yes." The Tooth King nodded. "He recorded the agreement that Frog Face, Gummy, and I made. The agreement that will change everything." He hesitated for a few minutes. "You should speak with

"He had numerous animals too."

Scribbles. Learn what you can from him—and protect him. Make sure the Blood-Spiller spills no more blood."

"But why?" Star asked. "Why is he after Gummy and Frog Face—and now Scribbles? What have they done that angered him?"

The Tooth King put a hand in the water and it came up wet. He splashed it across his face. "You were not asked to answer that question. Find the Blood-Spiller and kill him or bring him to me so I can have him killed. That's all. Now, you've done well, but your task isn't over. Stay close to Scribbles. I'll see to Gummy's protection." He sunk under the water before emerging again. "Is there anything else?"

"The Broadheads—" Star started.

"Broadheads? What about them?" Gummy gripped the edges and hauled himself out. He emerged naked, standing before us. Two servants brought a leopard skin, and he wrapped himself up.

Star looked at me. Perhaps she thought that it was better that I explain. Maybe it was. "You need the Flowering Fields for your—your plants." It felt ridiculous to say it. "But the Hill People need that land for their hunting. Especially because there are less animals in the hills." Because Thin Nose hunters wiped them away—but I didn't say that. "And then there's the Frost Clan. They want the Flowering Fields too."

The Tooth King listened carefully. A slave, a young woman with ash marks on her forehead, brought him a bowl of dried fruit, and he grabbed a fistful and tucked it into his mouth. "Well, we're there now, are we not? They'll have to seek game elsewhere."

"They'll go to war for their hunting grounds," Star said.

"Oh." The Tooth King cocked his head. "Red, you've lived with the Hillmen your whole life. You've seen the Frost Clan up close. Tell me truthfully, if there was a war, who do you think would win?"

I looked at the Tooth King, chewing on dried fruit, and then at Star. They had risked a lot for me. They had fought for me. But so had Song and Rock. Did I want to speak of their weaknesses to an enemy in a war that might be fought?

"You're nervous." The Tooth King bobbed his chubby head. "That's understandable. You might think you still have loyalty to the Hill Clan. That you owe them something. Again—understandable. But false." He reached over and patted my shoulder. "They cast you out. They called you weak. Your own father—he cursed you."

I froze. The talk of this put ice in my heart.

"And you came to me, starving. Your ribs sticking out. Another day and the Rider would have picked you up. And Red? You were so light, he could have lifted you with a finger and carried you up to the clouds." He smiled. "But then what happened?"

"You brought me in. You fed me. You cared for me."

"And made you a Fang. I do care for you. More than your father ever did, I'm certain of that." He gave the fruit bowl back to a slave. "So, I ask you—who would win?"

Star interrupted. "There doesn't have to be a war at all. Red talked with some of his friends in the Hill Clan." The words left her mouth in a torrent. "They're willing to share. A treaty can be created. And we know you're good at making agreements. Even the Frost People might be willing to talk—"

"I don't know about that. From what I've heard of the Frost Clan, they don't seem to enjoy talking."

"It's worth a try, O Tooth King," Star said. "Because if war does come, it doesn't matter who wins. Many Broadheads will die. Many people of the Heap will die. The Blood-Spiller will be nothing compared to that." She narrowed her eyes. "I know war. I know this."

A story from her past—something I knew almost nothing about.

He listened carefully. "You're right. I know war too. I know how fragile a place like the Heap can be." He nodded. "I'll send a messenger to the Hill Clan. Another to the Frost Clan. I will ask their leaders to come here and talk. A treaty will be forged." He hesitated. "But I want this Blood-Spiller caught. We must show strength—and a killer, bringing the Wrong Death to the Heap, does not belong in a place of strength. Do you understand?"

Star knelt. I knelt next to her. "Glory to the Tooth King!" We both called out in unison.

He clasped his hands. "Glory to the Fangs. Now do what I ask of you."

We left to do just that.

We descended. Away from the grand heights of the Heap's peak, past the finery that teeth brought, and made our way to the level above the Cave of the Gods. More pain to my bad leg. Scribbles, true to his name, worked in the Cave of the Scribes, and that's where we would find him. Star led the way, crossing a narrow bridge stretched across a gap in the cliffs, and to a jutting plateau next to the cave. A cluster of young Narrow Faces who wished to be scribes squatted together, their feet dangling off the edge, working on their arms or the stones below them with charcoal sticks while a crook-backed teacher watched.

Scribing—I didn't understand it.

Drawing made sense. Capture a beast, a demon, a spirit, a story in the crushed juice of berries, dried blood, and charcoal. Let it stand on stone, so you could see it with your eyes as well as hear it with your ears. The Hill People made many drawings. But these scribes didn't do that. They counted with lines—little etchings marked like tiger stripes on every available surface. And why? To record what their minds couldn't remember.

Like anything that couldn't be remembered was worth keeping in the first place.

Star led me past the young scribes and into the cave. Fat lamps burned along shelves worked into the walls, casting dancing flickering lights where the scribes worked. Thin, tired—their bodies pale, they worked tirelessly with their charcoal sticks. Scratching their lines onto the cave wall, on shards of pottery, and on their own arms and legs. I nearly tripped over one such scribe, who lay on his back, carefully copying marks from his belly to the stone wall above his head. He squawked as I mumbled an apology.

"What is the point of this?" I asked Star. "All this drawing."

"*Writing*," Star said—another Narrow Face word I didn't recognize. "It helps with counting. What do you when you want to count something and you run out of fingers?"

"I'll use my toes."

"You got ten of one and ten of the other. If you're lucky. That's twenty—that's not enough. There's much bigger numbers that have to be recorded. How many teeth are in a trade agreement for pelts, or jugs of fruit juice, or wolf pups. And if it's recorded, no one can cheat another. To claim that they already paid when they haven't—or if a pelt's got a hole in it and needs to be returned. This way, all the Heap can trade with safety."

"Maybe they should try not cheating each other."

Star sighed. "You're a good one, Red—but there are some things you just don't understand." She tapped the scribe with her feet. "Do you know where Scribbles is?"

He pointed with his stick to the end of the cave. That's where we went and where we found Scribbles.

He had a long strand of pale beard jutting from his pointed chin, wrapped around a stick tipped with charcoal—so that he'd always have something with which to draw. Countless lines formed dark bands around his chest, arms, and even the back of his neck. Right now, he stood with a boy who bore the same pale hair, though in thicker wafts. "That's it—that it." He had a hand on the boy's shoulder, guiding his hand. "Look at that. A good straight line." He hugged the boy, who had to be his son. "You would make the Monkey Boy proud with your cleverness!"

"I would?" The boy beamed.

"Oh, without a doubt." Scribbles handed him another stick. "Now, you may draw what you will. A trumpeting mammoth. A roaring bear. Or just some shapes. You've earned it." He faced us as the boy knelt down and started drawing on his own. "Red. Star. Two Fangs to greet me." He stroked his beard. "You didn't come to here to see my son's etchings, I believe."

"No." Star offered her hand and he clasped it. "There's been a killing. The Wrong Death. Given to Frog Face."

"I heard."

"We spoke with Gummy," I added. "Gummy, Frog Face—and the Tooth King. They planned together. Dreamed of finding seeds—of planting them. You recorded the details. Maybe you know more."

Scribbles' mouth opened and he started to speak—before the words caught in his throat and came out in a quick cough. His eyes went behind us—then reached down and caught his son's arm. "Come on, Little Scribbles. We have to leave. We'll go the Cook Cave, get some sweet berries."

"But I'm not done with my drawing!" Little Scribbles whined.

Scribbles knelt beside the boy. He grabbed the charcoal stick and made a few quick slashes—designs etched on the tan stone with one hand. Then he grabbed Little Scribbles' arm and pulled him closer. "You'll draw later. Those berries won't wait." He pulled the boy closer, brushing past Star and I.

"What are you doing?" Star demanded. "Are you running from a Fang, scribe?"

"A hundred apologies—the Gods must forgive me—but I have something to do in the Cook Cave. Someone to see." He tugged his son toward the door. Little Scribbles went without argument, recognizing what I recognized at that moment.

Scribbles was terrified.

The hot fear stench drifted off him, and he stumbled past us. I turned around and saw what had frightened him.

There, in the mouth of the cave, stood Raven. He had his black-feathered cape draped around him, looking, well, like a giant raven that had perched there, waiting for something to die. How long had he been there? Scribbles and Little Scribbles went right up to him. I moved to follow, to hear what they were talking about, when Star put a hand on my shoulder.

She shook her head. "He won't say a thing to us. Not while Raven's here. That's why he left."

"Would Raven hurt him?"

"I don't know. If Gummy paid him enough teeth, maybe." Star knelt down, to the edge of the wall. "Red, can you bring a lamp closer? I need to see something."

I stepped back, grabbed a fat lamp in a clay tray, and brought it closer. Flickering light shone over the drawing Scribbles had made, above the drawing of his son—a very nice trio of wooly rhinos wandering along a plain.

Scribbles' drawing looked different. A deer skull, a mammoth head, a pole set with oversized flowers, and a lump with a dark shade in it that had to be a cave. Above that, little dots that might be stars and a sliver that had to be the moon.

"The Hill Spirits have made him crazy," I said.

"No—it's a message."

"He didn't say anything."

"A message in the drawing." Star pointed. "Look here—all the symbols. That's the Elephant Mother, the Thunder Serpent, the Rider. That cave—the Cave of the Gods. And up there. Stars, and the moon."

"The night sky."

"He wants to meet us. At night, at the Cave of the Gods." Star used the mammoth robe sleeve to smudge up the etching. "Less people there. Barely anybody, if we go when the moon is high among the stars. And his son won't be with him. He must think it will be safer." She nodded to herself. "Tonight, then. The Cave of the Gods." She handed back the lamp. "Let's get back into the sunlight."

We walked back out. The young scribes hurried in behind their teacher, ready to start scribbling. They hurried past us and ran into the shadowed cave. Star and I remained outside, the cold sunlight drifting down. Wind blew cold from the north. The frost would be rolling in soon, and then the snow and everything that came with it. Star pulled her cloak tight around her.

"You go back to your cave and rest, Red." She gave me a little smile. "I'll do the same. Then I'll come get you around sunset and we'll see what Scribbles has to say."

"What has made him so scared?" I asked. "Raven? The Blood-Spiller?"

"We'll find out."

And we would. I wanted the truth of it, and the Blood-Spiller close to the edge of my club, the tip of my spear, and my hands. I could break him, hurt him—and then his fellow Night Demons would drag him down and it would be over. But the problem of the Broadheads and the Narrow Ones—that would remain. A problem I couldn't bludgeon.

I would just have to deal with it when the time came.

The sun would not set for a while. I went back to my cave, to give myself the meal that I'd needed since arriving in the Heap. I sent Mouse to the Cook Cave to fetch my favorites, while I played with Good Wolf and her pups and gave them more training. We munched some jerky together until Mouse returned, nearly weighed down by a big sack of food, all warmed and spiced from the Cook Cave's fires. I cleared aside a spot in my cave, leaned back on some soft cushions, set the meal on my belly and at my sides, and began eating.

First, three eggs. I cracked them open and swallowed, letting the yolk and the white run down my throat and spill over my lips. Some root vegetables, softened with steam followed. Then, strips of deer meat, well-spiced. I gobbled them up and tossed the chunks of fat—the few I didn't eat—to Good Wolf and her pups. All that was before a haunch of boar meat, still on the bone. I attacked that meat carefully, ripping free every strand, before snapping the bone in half and sucking down the marrow.

Always my favorite part.

Finally, dried fruit with sweet herbs, all in a slick sauce. I guzzled them down, put my hands behind my back, and whistled. Good Wolf and her pups surrounded me and gobbled down the crumbs that covered my chest and licked up the sauce on my lips and cheeks.

I cleaned my hands in their drool and wiped it on their fur. The perfect ending to a perfect meal.

Mouse watched from the doorway—probably the way cave lion cubs watched their parents eat. A mixture of awe and terror, and hunger for the scraps. She was welcome to them, along with the other bag of food she'd bought for herself. A reward for watching after Good Wolf tonight.

I stood and stretched. "The stars glow. The moon rises. I must go."

She had a rib, thick with meat, and gnawed on it as she wrapped a deerskin blanket around her shoulders. "Will you see him?" She lowered her voice. "The Blood-Spiller?"

My spear and club leaned against the wall. I took them both. "Maybe. And if we do, I'll kill him." If he could be killed—if he wasn't a Night Demon, who would catch arrows and shrug off spear stabs and laugh.

"Be careful," Mouse added.

I grunted. "I will. I want to come back to them." I patted Good Wolf. "And to you."

She smiled—strangely shy for Mouse. Then I went out into the darkness.

The Heap had only quieted a little during the night. Winter's chill kept people in their caves, huddled around fires, instead of traveling up and down the slopes or climbing the ladders in the last moments of twilight. One bonfire blazed on a rocky promontory near the bridge leading to the level of the Gods'

Cave, and had a decent crowd. They gathered together, huddled in their furs, and holding their hands over the fire.

Listening to Tale-Spinner telling one of her stories. "The Blood-Spiller—a man of flesh and blood or a monster, cast out of the underworld for being too cruel!" She had some of her helpers behind her, one working a drum in a regular rhythm, the other, a hunchback hoisting up little statues as she talked. Acting out her words. "He appeared in the woods. Sliding out of the shadows. Ready to kill again!"

A puppet of the Blood-Spiller. A creation of dark fur and a monkey skull, dangling from gut strings. Spinner's friend swung the puppet over the fire, shifting the smoke and making the audience gasp.

"But two Fangs—the beauty from far away, who wields a weapon made from a star, and the giant, heroic Broadhead, who speaks the language of beasts—rose up to stand against him!" She motioned to her helper.

Two more puppets joined the fray. One had been constructed of dark wood, with a shining spear of quartz in one hand. The other had been made from the stuffed body of a badger, with shining stone eyes and a stick in the place of a spear. What was she doing with those? Wait—the one with the quartz. Was that Star? And that meant—the badger was me? I touched my chest. Was I really so big, compared to the Thin Noses?

"The Broadhead Beast-Man can speak to animals, but the Blood-Spiller can summon them as well. He calls the mammoths to attack the heroes." She opened her hand, letting loose a fistful of powdered ash. It ran down. The hunchbacked helper dropped the Blood-Spiller and drew out another puppet. A mammoth, made of squirrel fur with carved sticks for tusks. "But the Broadhead has unstoppable strength. They battle!" The two puppets—the mammoth and me—swung together and crashed.

That wasn't how it happened. I didn't fight the mammoths—I ran from them. And I certainly couldn't speak to animals. They spoke their own language. But the Narrow Ones around the fire loved it. They stared in rapt attention, their eyes wide and reflecting the dancing firelight.

Spinner glanced at me over the blaze. She smiled and gave a quick nod. I snorted and went on my way. We had told her the truth and she had turned it into a legend. Let her do that. I had other things to worry about. I traveled up the slope, turned the corner, and reached the Cave of the Gods.

The light had faded here, the numerous fires that usually danced around the altars and statues flickering their way down into only embers before they vanished entirely. A few shamans and worshippers milled about, setting down their final offerings or whispering their last prayers to the Monkey Boy, the Thunder Snake, or the Elephant Mother, before going on their way. I strolled among the statues of those Narrow One Gods until I spotted Star, standing in the mouth of the big cave—where the shamans had prepared Frog Face for burial.

I walked over and joined her.

"Where is Scribbles?"

Star shrugged. "No here yet. Must be waiting for the sky to grow darker."

"Hmmm." I shrugged. "I walked by one of Spinner's fires. The story she was telling."

"I saw one outside the Cook Cave. Her and her band have them on all over the Heap. Making a good profit of teeth as well." She gripped tight to the strap over her cloak. "I should never have told her. But she puts flowers around my heart and my head gets soft."

"The puppet of you looked pretty," I said. "The puppet of me was a dead badger."

"Truly—the real Red is much better." She grinned slyly and I grinned back. Then Star nudged me and pointed. "Look. By the Rider."

Scribbles stood next to the statue of the God of Death. He wore a black bearskin and a fur cap, shifting his footing and walking in uneasy circles around the statue. Occasionally looking up at the skull emerging from its blanket, like the Rider would lean down and whisper comforting words into his ear.

"Let's go," Star said.

We crossed the stone. Now, the plateau was nearly empty. We passed the statue of the Thunder Snake, with its shimmering scales and stones, and reached Scribbles. He had his hands in the pockets of his cloak. "Red. Star." He gave us each a quick nod. "You weren't followed? You're certain of it? Swear on all the Gods that you weren't."

"Don't put ice in your words—we weren't followed." Star leaned closer. "Were you?"

He winced. "I don't know."

"Well, tell us what you wanted to tell us," I asked. "Tell us about Gummy, and the Tooth King, and Frog Face."

"They think—they think I won't tell you all of it. That's what Raven told me, when we met earlier."

"Did he threaten you?" Star asked.

"He *is* a threat. But not compared to—to the other one. The one you call the Blood-Spiller."

"Do you know who he is?" I asked.

He opened his mouth, but Star shouted first. She grabbed Scribbles and hurled him to the side—just as an arrow hummed through the air. It plunged into Star's shoulder, the point driving down into her cloak. A rasping scream escaped her clenched teeth and she tumbled down. Scribbles shrieked. I stared past Star, looking further up the slope.

Moonlight, shining on a stone arrowhead. Bright in the darkness.

"Red—get him out of here!" Star cried as she rolled over, the arrow still projecting up from her shoulder-blades. Was there death in that arrow? Had the Wrong Death come to Star?

I wanted to ignore Scribbles. To charge the Blood-Spiller and end him.

"Red!" Star repeated. "Protect Scribbles—he's the quarry!"

Protect Scribbles. Star would be safe as the Blood-Spiller hunted Scribbles.

I grabbed Scribbles and hauled him away. Running from Star. We dashed around the length of the statue. The arrow whistled behind him, humming down and landing in the statue. It settled amongst the Rider's ribcage. Like the Blood-Spiller was taking aim at death itself.

Star remained in the statue's shadow, curled up by the altar. The Blood-Spiller—like any good hunter—was separating his prey. She looked up at me and Scribbles, pain in her eyes, clutching the wound, fingers around the shaft poking up from the back of her shoulder. I had to get Scribbles to safety and get back to her.

Where to hide? "There!" I pointed ahead. A narrow cave opening. The place where the Rider's worshippers kept their holy bones. At least it would get us out of the open. I pushed Scribbles. "Move!"

Broadhead strength made him move faster. We hurried into the cave.

Bones everywhere. Skeletons rested thickly on the wall. Animal bones. Perhaps some Narrow One skeletons had been mixed in as well, but it was hard to tell in the lowlight. Bones hung from the ceiling, wheeling slightly in the cold wind, and covered the wall. Some cleaned and white and shining, others brown with dust. Scribbles and I slid past dangling chains of bones, and neared the end of the cave.

We stayed still. Surrounded by silence, apart from our ragged breathing. I could get the Blood-Spiller with my spear as he came closer—maybe.

"Red, I have to tell you—I have to tell you the truth." Scribbles stammered to get the words out. "Gummy, Frog Face, the Tooth King—there was a fourth."

Something clicked in front of us. Someone else moving through the bones.

I raised a finger and put it in front of Scribbles' lips. He went silent.

The click came again. Pushing aside another bone chain. My spear wouldn't work here. Too close. I let it rest on the wall and drew my club. A few blows, backed with Broadhead strength, and I'd shatter the mask of the Blood-Spiller—then the rest of him as well. I stepped in front of Scribbles, moving to protect him.

"The Broadhead Fang." Another voice. A gentleness to it. Like a whisper, though the volume was loud. "Red."

He knew me. That wasn't odd. Everyone knew everyone in the Heap. Had we ever spoken to each other? Had we joked? Shared a haunch of meat around a fire?

I gripped the club with both hands. "Come closer."

"I like you. I drip honey in my words for you, Red." The ape skull. It emerged amongst the bone. Next to me, Scribbles moaned. "I like all Broadheads. I watched them and talked to them whenever they came to the Heap to trade. They are free, out there in the woods, and the hills, and mountains. They know true happiness. You know, I would die right now, if I could be reborn a Broadhead."

"Come closer," I repeated. "And I'll talk about being a Broadhead all you want."

"Yes." The skull mask shifted. "We will."

A rush of wind. Something pinched me, where my neck met my chest. My finger went up. A wooden dart, piercing my skin. A line of blood dripped down. A black line in the low light. I pulled free the needle and stared at it.

The bones blurred. The world started to spin. Night Demons danced at the corner of my vision. They'd come crawling out and drag me away. Carry me to the land of nightmares.

I had to hold on. I stepped closer and swung the club. It smashed against bones before slipping from my grasp. No—I had to be stronger. I reached for it, only for my legs to vanish. I hit the cave floor instead and lay there.

"No…" Scribbles behind me, crying. "Please—I have children…."

"I'm doing this for them." That skull loomed closer. Big as the sun. "And for all the children of mankind. It will hurt me to do this, just as much as it hurts you. I beg you to forgive me. Your friends never gave me a choice."

Then the darkness carried me into the land of dreams.

The Hill Spirits ruled the dreams. They carried you away when you slept and showed you their world—or your own memories, but twisted like a reflection in a pond split with ripples. But too often, the Spirits weren't the ones to reach you. The Night Demons did. This is what happened now. They sent me racing through the forest, wrapped in snow. They made the starving pain erupt in my stomach. They showed the Heap, covered in ice and abandoned. Scavenging hyenas playing amongst the bodies of dead Narrow Ones and Broadheads alike.

The carnage from a war.

Then they opened my mouth and poured in the dirt.

I awoke with a gasp. There was something in my mouth. A bundle of sinew and hide. More strings around it, holding the gag in place. Thick leather tying my arms and legs together. My bad ankle hurt worse than ever. I tugged at the ropes. Broadhead strength—maybe that would help.

"Stop it." The Blood-Spiller's voice. We were somewhere dark and small. A little cave. Only a few fat lamp torches blazed in the corners. They shone on the Blood-Spiller himself as he walked closer. He had shed the cloak, but still wore the ape skull mask. The skin, strangely pale in the light of the lamps. Like he was some cave creature, who had never known the sun. He carried a short-handled axe—a fine weapon, the polished stone held tightly in place and carvings of snarling beasts along the shaft. "Stop it, Red."

I grunted and tugged at the bonds on my wrists even more.

"Stop it!" An almost childish whine in his words.

I didn't stop. He hit me with the axe handle, a glancing backhand blow to the side of my head. Some strength behind the blow. The skull loomed closer. Then I stopped struggling.

Yes—he truly was a Night Demon.

"You don't understand." He stepped back. "If you did, you would agree with what I was doing. You'd praise me. You and all the Broadheads—you'd help me, and your spears would join the work of my knife."

I let my eyes tell him of my hate.

"I'm going to keep you gagged. Just for a moment." He leaned closer. His eyes, visible in the sockets of his mask. "I mean you no harm. But I can't risk you yelling. Besides, I need to talk and I don't want to be interrupted." He reached past me. Was he going to draw out his knife? The blade that he had used to kill Frog Face?

That he had perhaps already used to give poor Scribbles the Wrong Death?

Instead, he brought back a seed. He held it up to my nose. Would that seed be placed in mouth, along with fistfuls of dirt? Would the thick taste coat my tongue, and spill down my throat, and choke me as his knife slipped between my ribs?

Maybe that had already happened to Scribbles.

"You know what this is?" He pulled the seed away.

I grunted.

"Oh—you can't speak. Yes—I forgot. I am very foolish sometimes." He

"You don't understand."

patted my cheek, almost friendly. Why was he doing this? Why hadn't he given me the Wrong Death while I slept? "Well, the seed is the future. No—*a* future. It is what *might* be. But it is a different future. Your friend, Autumn, she must have told you about it. The way she talks about the growing times to come, about fields of wonderful plants, juicy fruits hanging from the vine. Oh—it is good to hear." He nodded his head. "I wouldn't mind biting into her. Letting the juice run down my cheeks. If you know the meaning of my words."

I grunted louder and tugged at my bonds.

"Stop it!" He raised. "Stop, or I'll hit you again."

I stopped.

He had me in his power. Just like the Night Demons when they ruled my dreams. He could do whatever he wanted.

CHAPTER FOUR
A BROADHEAD SEEKS LOVE

The Blood-Spiller—the Night Demon—moved his hand to my mouth. "I'm going to remove the leather in your mouth. You'll be a good Broadhead." Should I go for his fingers? Maybe I could catch some in my teeth. Snap them off. But then what? That would just put fire in his heart and he'd bring the axe down, right on my skull. "Tell me that you'll be a good Broadhead. Do that for me, Red—before I go further."

I grunted.

"I want to hear the flowers in your words." He gripped the bundle and tugged as he pulled the axe back. "Tell me you'll be a good Broadhead or I'll give you the Wrong Death right here!" His voice went shrill and echoed through the caves. Then he tore out the gag.

"I will be a good Broadhead." I murmured the words.

"I'll make sure you do." He reached to a basket dangling from the ceiling on a gut-string line and drew out a thorn—the edge glistening in some juice that caught the torchlight's gleam. "This will help you make the right choice." He reached over and jabbed it into my shoulder. A little poke—the kiss of a thorn. Compared to all the aches this night had given me, it was nothing. "It will take a while. But that will give me all the time I need—and it will help my words as well. I made the juice that I soak the darts myself. It will make you travel, Red. Don't worry. Let it happen."

It was like when I had eaten the mushrooms in Mother Rat's cave. The ones that only shamans should eat, to let the Narrow One Gods scrape the insides of their skulls with magic fingers. As the Blood-Spiller moved back, he started to shimmer. The dirty white of his mask bulged and shifted and melted, and night clung to his pale skin. A Night Demon stood before me, gesturing with his axe toward the opening of the cave—which drew closer and widened into a hungry mouth lined with more teeth than I could ever count.

"I want you to imagine Autumn's future. Though, truthfully, it is Gummy's future. And even more truthfully, it belongs to the Tooth King." The cave opened wide. "All those trees. The fruit in the branches and the roots in the earth. Do you think they'll grow easily, as they do in the wild? Do you think we can just reach out and pluck one—and that will be the end of the gathering like it is now? No. We'll bring the plants water. We'll work the soil to feed them. We'll chase away pests. We'll break our backs gathering. And still it won't be enough."

What was he talking about? Where was Scribbles? The world pulsed as light shifted.

"See it, Red. Imagine this future—when we are slaves to the soil."

Then I saw it. Through the eye of the cave mouth. Row upon row of trees, berry bushes, and roots. Ropes winding from them, to the thin arms of slaves. The sun beat down and the day went on, and still they toiled. They worked endlessly, resting only a little before rising up to do it again and again and again—to make piles of fruit, roots, and berries grow bigger.

And around them, villages grew. The Heap, swollen like a bad wound. Houses and tents along its slopes, and into its forests—which vanished to clear away more land for growing places. They were like a tick, jaws wedged deep into the flesh of the earth. Growing fatter and fatter as they sucked.

"We'll grow more numerous. More food means more mouths—which means that there must be more food. On and on. Growing endlessly. Serving the dirt." The Blood-Spiller popped into my vision, holding up a shining seed—the same one he had put in Gummy's mouth. "Serving the seeds. And it will never end."

Once again, I opened my mouth to argue. Maybe this was true. Maybe the future of slavery to the soil would be bad. But was the Wrong Death the right response? Killing Gummy, sending mammoths to trample me, and capturing me and Scribbles—what would that create but more pain?

"I see what you're thinking." The Blood-Spiller tapped his skull-mask. "Is it worth it? Is what I've done—what I will do—worth it?" He patted my cheek. "Consider your people. Consider the Broadheads. See what the future holds for them."

The hills loomed and the mountains beyond. The caves lay empty. The fires gone. Our tools and spears unused in the dirt, our paintings and totems to the

Hill Spirits dusty and forgotten.

Only bones remained. Half-buried, and gray with age. Scattered in the snow or in the corner of our caves.

"You will vanish from the earth." The Blood-Spiller whispered in my ear—though I couldn't see him. Only the dancing, warped image of the bones and the growing dust. "When the Thin Ones grow numerous, even your strongest warriors can't stop them. Full of their grown food, they'll overwhelm you. And then you will be nothing but bones, and then a story, and then not even that."

A moan crept up. I had left the Hill People. I had run from them, and joined the Heap. Would they be gone because of me?

"What will they say, when they find your skeletons? The children of the children of the children of the Thin Noses. What will they imagine?" He made his voice grand and booming—a storyteller's voice. "Look at these monsters, who our hero fathers met in battle and destroyed? Look at these sad creations. Mistakes made by the Gods. A mercy, that they are all gone. But it won't matter. No Broadhead ears will hear it."

"N-no…" I managed a word—and barely that.

"And why? Why all this pain—for my kind and for yours?" The Blood-Spiller sounded very close by. Enough so that his tongue could scrape my ear. "I will show you. See, who we labor for. See what it builds."

I gazed upon an ocean of teeth.

More than I could ever imagine. A sea of white and yellow, pressed together and stacked. Useless, away from their mouths. A pointless gathering. In the middle, on an island of colored stone, sat the Tooth King. Fatter than when I had last seen him. More sparkling stones worked into his fat. Graying hair and wrinkles mixing with his flab. He waved his hands, and waves coursed through the teeth. The clatter, deafening.

"Many will work in those fields. Many will gather the plants. But who will benefit? Kings. The rich. They will do no work at all, except for giving commands. And yet, they and their children will rule. They'll cover the world in seeds, and wipe away everything that does not give them wealth. And for that wealth, the world will die."

He appeared in front of me. With his skull, he could have been the Rider, the Thin Nose God of Death—arriving to drag us away, as a final punishment for what we had done to the world.

For what I was doing, right there, by helping the Heap against the Blood-Spiller.

A sudden, stinging slap. The vision faded. My journey ended. Once again, I was back in the cave, hidden away in shadow, and looking at the Blood-Spiller. He slapped me again.

"Do you see?" He stepped back. "You may speak, Red. The juices I gave you, they should be fading. Not enough so that you can move, but so you can speak."

Sure enough, when I moved my lips, words left them. "That was—that was what will happen?" My voice came hoarse, like my tongue had forgotten how to move. "That is the future? What will come when those seeds go into earth?"

"That's why I do what I do," the Blood-Spiller said. "It is what the Gods demand. To remove the curse of seeds, I must plant seeds inside of those who would plant."

That explained how he killed—and where he put the seeds. But how did he know about this? How could he have hunted Frog Face so easily?

Maybe he was a Night Demon after all.

I grunted. "Tell them. Tell the others."

"You don't think I have? I have spoken until I could speak no more. Gummy, Frog Face—the Tooth King. They don't listen. They see the teeth they'll find, the Thin Noses waited to be born and fed, and every other worry vanishes from their heads. Besides, the Gods chose me to act. Not to talk."

He grabbed a wooden bowl and pressed it to my lips. For a moment, I recoiled—but it was only water. Cool, clear river water. Welcome as it rushed down over my lips and into my throat. Giving me some strength back.

"You are chosen by them, then?" I asked.

He bobbed his masked head. "Who else would speak to me?"

Night Demons. That was who.

Because the visions might be true, and the future may end in doom for the Broadheads, but the Blood-Spiller was not a good warrior. No one who gave out the Wrong Death like he did, slaughtering and mutilating, could be a good warrior. If there was a way to fight this bad future, it couldn't be with knives slipped between ribs and mouths filled with dirt.

I groaned. "Where is Scribbles?"

"Scribbles the scribe." The Blood-Spiller hesitated. "Do not worry about Scribbles the scribe. Worry about what you're going to do. I am going to cut you free and then ask you a question. Answer in the right way, and you'll keep breathing."

He reached the cluttered wall, to the wooden shelf where he kept all his strange tools. The beautifully-crafted axe slid neatly back into its place. He returned with a dagger—an equally impressive weapon. The stone had been carefully worked into a lethal point, and he had delicate carvings along the handle and pommel. He hoisted it up, letting the smoky light of the torches play amongst them. Animals running. Figures hoisting spears. A hunter's knife, showing a hunt.

Was this the blade that had killed Frog Face? That may have already given the Wrong Death to Scribbles?

The Blood-Spiller lunged. For a moment, it looked like he was going to plunge that blade into my gut. Instead, he slipped behind me and cut the ropes holding back my arms. I dropped down, falling from the wall and landing on the earth. The cold stone struck against me—a bad embrace. Dirt clung to my hair and fingers.

"Will you stand in my way, Red? In my war, there are only two sides. Which will you be on?"

He was asking before I had the strength to stand—or that's what he thought. But when I asked my knees to move, they did. My toes wiggled and my muscles slid slightly. Just a little. I could stand—maybe. But I might as well try flying as running. Maybe the liquid coating the needle had been made for Narrow Face bodies, and not for Broadheads, so I recovered faster than he planned.

Or maybe the Hill Spirits had helped me.

Either way, I had a chance.

I folded up my fingers. He had the knife in his hand and the short axe on the shelf next to him. I could barely stand. It would be a short fight—if I chose to stay.

"Well?" He leaned closer. "Tell me your answer, Red?"

My fist gave him his answer, as it drove against his chin and knocked him back. A wild blow—but when you have Broadhead strength, you don't have to hit a Thin Nose hard to hurt them. He went back and crashed into the shelf. It crumbled. Pots and jugs shattered. Insects boiled out. Centipedes, spiders, and scorpions tumbled down, spilling over our bodies, their little forms black and shining in the firelight.

As he retched, I stood. He got the knife up and managed a clumsy stab, just as I rammed past him with everything I had. I tumbled past him, as his blade carved a trail up my arm and onto my shoulder. Bright blood sprayed against the walls. The stinging came—a burn that made me yell. My cry echoed through the cave as I slammed my other arm against him.

Pushing him against the stone. Holding him in place.

The knife came again. A wicked slice, against my side now. Trying to get through my ribs. I stumbled back first, put a hand on the cut, and put my knee into his belly. His mouth opened and a gasping, rattling noise crept from the skull-mask.

I could stay. Rip the mask. See the face beneath. The Spirits know that I'd probably recognize him.

But if I stayed a second longer, he'd put that blade in my throat.

Instead, I spun, arms flailing, and ran out of the cave.

A hide covering over the exit. Hiding it from sight. I burst through, ripping my way into the night air. The cold pressed against my skin. My mammoth fur cloak—the Blood-Spiller had taken it, leaving only my deerskins. Frost settled on the forest grasses, and stabbed painfully into my feet. The cold reached into my lungs, stabbing against me with each breath.

I couldn't stop to look. Couldn't stop to find where exactly the Blood-Spiller had made his cave. Otherwise, he would take that fine bow of wood, antler, and sinew, and put an arrow in my back.

So I ran on. Water splashed in the distance. A bubbling stream, swollen with snowmelt. I tried to run to that.

The Hill Spirits had other ideas.

They put a big rock in my foot and I banged my toes in it—then they made the hill lift up and swung it over my head, and under me, and over again. I was tumbling down. Falling and rolling. After all this, I would fall down and meet my end that way.

I shouldn't have been surprised. The Hill Spirits like funny deaths.

The fall ended. They put something else in front of me. I collided with it and then they swept me up and carried me into the night sky and I saw nothing more.

Something soft and wet tickled my face. My eyes flicked open. I looked up to see Good Wolf's big eyes, luminous in the dawn. She bopped my face with her nose and continued licking, her tail wiggling wildly and her whole body shaking. Was I back in my cave? Was the battle with the Blood-Spiller just another dream-journey, that the Hill Spirits had taken me on when I slept, before bringing me safely back before I woke up?

Then I raised my arm, and sudden pain burned its way up to my shoulder.

No dream at all.

"Hold still, hold still!" Bug Eyes' rasp. He crouched next to me, working with bone needle and gut string. It pinched and ached and I tried not to wail. "Just a little more, Red. Oh, Thunder Serpent, I beg of you—give me your strength. It's like trying to heal a mammoth." Watching him didn't help matters. I turned my head the other way. If I couldn't see, maybe it wouldn't hurt so much.

I looked at Star instead.

She crouched next to me, worry lining her face. Good Wolf had pawed over and sat next to her, and she idly rubbed her hand along the length of the dog's back. "She found you, Red." She patted Good Wolf's head, flattening her ears. "Got your scent from your cave and then we followed her out into the woods." She glanced at Bug Eyes. "Ready?"

"A moment more." He leaned closer to my arm, and his mouth opened, showing off all the welts and sores from the bugs he lived with. For a moment, I imagined he was going to bite into my arm and I tried to pull it back, but his thin, strong fingers held it in place. He bit into the gut string, and snapped it apart. "There. Now I must whisper a prayer to the Rider—beg of him to slow his hooves. To let this one stay on the earth a moment longer."

"You'll have to say the prayer as we move." Star pointed to a tree. "Look where we are."

A skull had been placed in a low-hanging branch, all its flesh picked clean. The mouth gaped open—screaming still. A flower had been placed in that mouth, with more set in a garland around the branch. Two flowers, bright purple, had been placed in the eyes. A bit of brilliant color next to the whiteness of bone.

Fresh flowers. The mark of the Eaters.

"We're in Eater land?" I asked.

Star took my shoulder and helped me to my feet. She grunted with the strain. "Yes. Lucky none of their scouts have found us yet. Or they might be eating you up as we speak." We walked to the edge of the clearing, Bug Eyes shaking and humming his prayer as Good Wolf let a yip and trotted at my side. Star pointed. "Brought your belongings."

My spear and my club. My mammoth fur cloak. It was good to have them back. And the necklace of the tiger's tooth. A fang for a Fang. That, I still had.

I slid on the cloak and took up my weapons. "The Blood-Spiller. He has a cave here. He brought me to it. Talked to me." Should I tell her what he said? What I saw? A future of endless labor for the Thin Ones, and doom for the Broadheads? No—that would make her as confused as me. "He put a strange juice into me. Then I broke free. I fell down a slope." I stared through the trees. Mist everywhere, and cold clinging to the ground. "It was—no—it has to be—"

Where was that slope? Where was that cave?

"He made his home in Eater Territory," Star said. "Cunning. He knows that if we spend too long searching the hills, the Eaters will find us. He's probably hidden from them—or he made some kind of deal." Evil clung to evil. Night Demons loved the company of other Night Demons. "Very Cunning."

"Did you recognize him?" Bug Eyes asked. "See his face?"

"The mask stayed on. I think...I think he has nothing under it. That skull is his face."

"Maybe." Star shrugged. "When we find him, we'll find out." She pointed through the trees. "This way. Back to the trail."

Lingering in Eater Territory was a good way to end up in an Eater's belly. We kept moving, hurrying through the trees and the mist. The cloak helped with the cold, and though my arm and shoulder burned, the cut hadn't been deep. It would heal.

Unlike some wounds that Blood-Spiller had made.

"What about Scribbles?" I caught up to Star—no easy task, with her long legs. "Did you find him after—"

"No." She stopped and looked away. "He vanished. Just like you."

And the Blood-Spiller might already have given him the Wrong Death.

"It doesn't make sense." Star muttered to herself as she loped along. Up ahead, a wide trail meandered through the forest, passing several rocks already slick with ice. "How he could move so fast? Picking you up and carrying you away—dropping you off here in Eater territory? It's like he turned into a great bird and took you in his talons."

"Are you asking me?" I wondered. "I don't know."

She gave me a smile. "Putting my thoughts into words, Red. Nothing more."

"Thin One foolishness." Then, I had another question. "Are we searching for Scribbles?" That would be the right thing to do. His son—his family. They'd want him found, no matter if he was alive or dead. Even if it meant straying into the Eaters' part of the Bloodwood.

Bug Eyes drew closer, coughing and stumbling. "Wait—wait for me." He paused and rested his hands on his knees, his chest heaving. Shamans could fly around with the help of their mushrooms, but they still needed legs to run—and Bug Eyes' legs were weak. Her perked up as Good Wolf sniffed him curiously. "No time to search for the scribe. We'll send more Fangs into the woods when we get back."

"Back from what?"

Star patted my shoulder. "The Tooth King listened to us. So did the Broadheads. They're sending a group to meet us at the Mother's Heart, to talk about what comes next." To avoid war, and so much Wrong Death that would result. "The King's already left, with many of his followers. They're waiting for us in the Flowering Fields, before moving on to the Tusk Lands." A desolate place, home to the mammoth herds. Set just about between the Heap and the hills and mountains where my people lived. "The Hill People will meet us there. And the Frost Clan too. And the Tooth King wants you along."

It made sense. Others spoke in the way that Broadheads speak and in the way that Thin Ones speak, but none were as loyal to the Tooth King as me.

But the fear crept back to me—the fear that had emerged, cold and flickering, in the Tooth King's cave the day before. The simple question about what would happen if there was war between the Heap and the Broadheads. If the blood started to flow, from the hills and mountains, through the forest, across the fields, and all the way to the Heap—who would I fight for? Where did I belong?

"Red." Bug Eyes stepped closer to me. I towered over him. The top of his bird-mask barely scraped my shoulder. "You're worried—there's a battle in you. Between Thin Nose and Broadhead. Your home and where you were born." He took my hand, clasped it in his. "But if we succeed, you won't have to choose. There will be peace."

"Peace," I agreed. "Yes. Then it's good you asked for me. The Tooth King will need me by his side."

"I need you by my side," Star said. "Let's go."

We continued down the trail, heading for the Fields.

Peace—but that wasn't what I'd seen in the Blood-Spiller's cave. In that world, the bones of the Broadheads lay heavy on the mountainside. We were all gone, replaced by the Thin Noses, with the bellies of their children swollen by the plants they grew. And my people would vanish like the mist under the heat of the sun.

No—those were lies of the Blood-Spiller. Force them away and help your friends.

I continued on through the forest.

The sun was high when we reached the Flowering Fields, but it hadn't done much against the cold. Flecks of snow drifted down, catching the sun as they flitted and danced their way to the grass and flowers. The Hill Spirits had a cruel sense of humor. They enjoyed combining the dangerous with the beautiful.

The men of the Heap rested in the field, the Feathers standing at attention along the edge of the road with their plumed spears at their sides. Some of the other wealthy of the Heap, the Tooth King's advisors, squatted on the grass or snacked on spiced jerky or roots—enjoying the respite from the journey. Autumn knelt at the edge of the stream that ran through the Flowering Fields, collecting water in a set of clay jugs that went onto her belt. She was probably glad to be back, where she could continue her work and her learning.

And at the center of it all, the Tooth King sat on his litter, his slaves resting around him. He had brought his cave hyenas too, and he threw them chunks of bone—which they caught and broke with snaps of their jaws.

Star and I maneuvered through the crowd and came to his side while Bug Eyes wandered into the grass to talk with Autumn—I didn't like that. What did they have to talk about? Good Wolf growled at the hyenas, who made their cackles and snarls. I snapped my fingers and pointed to the ground. Good Wolf went to her belly—flattening herself even as the hyenas cackled louder. That was good. I didn't want her fighting with the Tooth King's pets.

Then Star and I dropped to the ground ourselves. "Glory to the Tooth King!" We shouted it together.

The Tooth King brought us to our feet with a wave of his hand. "The Gods are kind to you, Red. And to me as well. I feared you were gone—and yet, here you are." One of the cave hyenas scampered over and set its huge head in the Tooth King's lap. It looked absurd, but the Tooth King was like a Hill Spirit made flesh. Why shouldn't even these beasts listen to him? "What happened? Do we know the Blood-Spiller's name?"

"He—he kept on his mask." I wish I could tell him more. "He wants the planting to stop. That's why he killed Frog Face, and put the seed in his mouth. A message—a warning. To stop your plans."

Something flashed in the Tooth King's eyes. "He gives the Wrong Death to my friends to send me a message? He should try putting flowers in his words. I have heard his message, and I'll give him one of my own before I let him die." The hyena let out a low, pleased rumble. A growl or a purr—I couldn't tell. "But that will have to wait. Child Who Catches Falling Stars—did you tell him about our purpose here?"

"I did, O Tooth King," Star answered. "But I ask you, what about Gummy? The Blood-Spiller wants him, doesn't he? And why does he want him? And then there are the others—like Autumn."

Autumn. My eyes went to her. Would she be in danger?

"That is not a question you need to ask." The Tooth King shrugged as Star squinted. "Gummy has Raven to look after him. And my mind is free from worries when I think of Gummy. If you place your hand in a monster's mouth, you should not be surprised when you are bitten." What did that mean? A monster? But the Tooth King had already moved on. "We'll rest for a few moments. Then we go on, to the Mother's Heart. I'll need you, Red—so push aside fears of the Blood-Spiller. We go to build something better."

"Peace," I said. Repeating Bug Eyes' words.

"The future," the Tooth King replied. He settled back on his carved throne as he scratched the hyena behind the ears. "Go and rest."

When the Tooth King told you to rest, you rested.

Star and I walked to the stream's edge. Autumn perked up and hurried to me, a smile splitting her freckled face—bright as the sun. She wrapped her arms around me. "You made it, Red—you're well." She settled down, and the smile vanished. Replaced with a bright redness in her cheeks. "I was—I was worried."

"I was worried too," I agreed. Why was she putting such bright flowers around her words? "The Wrong Death was close. But I didn't get it."

Star cleared her throat. "The journey to the Mother's Heart promises to be long. We could use some berries to eat—and not dried ones either, which sometimes taste like they fell out of Good Wolf's behind." She pointed to a cluster of bushes further up the stream. "Autumn, Red—maybe you could gather some?"

"Berries are a good treat," I agreed. "Star, Bug Eyes—you should go with us."

"I'll be busy." Star nudged Bug Eyes, who had been crouching down and examining something tiny in the grass. "So will Bug Eyes."

"Busy doing what?" I asked.

But then, Autumn grabbed my arm and pulled. I was bigger than her, with thicker legs, and it should have been like a fox trying to pull a tree. But when Autumn tugged at my arm, my feet followed. I trotted after her. We walked down the river, away from the others, and up a slight hillock to where the berries rested in the sun. They grew thick on the vines, but wouldn't last long thanks to the cold. Autumn produced one of the many little baskets from her cloak, and began pulling them free and plopping them in with an amazing speed.

I did my best to help.

She chuckled. "You're not a very good gatherer, Red."

"Maybe I should pull out the entire bush. Just carry it under my arm. I wouldn't mind the thorns."

"But then, it would be uprooted and no berries would ever grow again." She hesitated, a berry frozen midway between the plant and the basket. "Fear has put its venom into your heart, Red. About going to visit the Broadheads. Just like you were worried the night before, when we joined your kinsmen from the Hill Clan here in the field."

Now, a warmth crept into my cheeks. "Fear's venom is far from my heart."

"No. It is close." She stood up, the basket at her side. "But that's all right. Sometimes, it is good that fear is close. It's a warning. It tells us how we really feel. And you fear seeing the Broadheads again." Her voice lowered. "Were they—were they cruel to you?"

Cruel. Was that the word? I didn't know. Was the wolf cruel when it brought down the deer? Were the seasons cruel when they changed and the wind blew cold? That was just what happened. The clan had rules and I had broken them.

"I am—an outcast." The words stuck to my tongue and clicked against my teeth. Autumn wanted to help. I had to force them out. "I left the Hill People and I can never return. That's why I'm in the Heap. I became an outcast, and went down into the Bloodwood. That's where the Tooth King's scouts found me. They brought me back, and he healed me, and fed me, and cared for me. He made me part of the Heap."

"Why—why were you forced from the Hills?"

I looked down at my feet. "I was weak."

Just as I had been earlier, in the Blood-Spiller's cave. Too weak to fight him, or even stand against him. Too weak to do anything but run.

Autumn reached up with her hand. She tapped the bottom of my chin and pointed my face upwards, to meet her eyes. "I don't think you're weak at all. You certainly weren't the night when we were here. You stood alone against a herd of mammoths, and saved me by telling me to get to safety. And, as for being an outcast…" She hesitated. "It's not the same for me. I've grown up in the Heap. But because I think about things, because I question things—ask about the workings of the world—I find that I am apart as well."

"Apart?"

"Who else would ask what makes the sun shine? Or why grass grows where it does? Or why animals act the way they do?" She tapped her head. "Many people think the Gods have touched my brain. But not like the shamans. In a bad way. Making me ask too many questions."

I folded thick fingers into a fist. "Those people are wrong."

She laughed a little at that. "You say it so simply."

"Simple things are often true."

"Oh, Red." She put her hands on my chin and cheeks and stood on her tiptoes. "I am glad you came to the Heap."

Her lips pressed against mine. I held her close and kissed her back. Fire in her lips, and below her coat—so warm compared to the cold all around us.

She dropped the basket of berries.

We'd have to pick them up before we rejoined the others.

The procession moved north. We skirted the edge of the Flowering Fields— the flowers just starting to die under the onslaught of frost—and passed the herds of aurochs grazing carefully, mist around their muzzles, before the trail wound through a final patch of forest and then into the Tusk Lands. This was where mammoths dwelled, and every so often we would see their shapes looming in the distance—males who had left the herd and wandered alone. A gray country. Snow, dirtied, on spires of stone jutting up from the earth. Further up, the hills waited. A cold place, where the mist never really seemed to part.

My old home.

Beyond that, the mountains lifted tall and terrible. Covered with the pitiless frost. To dwell in a place like that, you had to be as hard as the stone underneath your feet. The Frost Clan certainly met that challenge. War came as naturally to them as hunting and gathering. They loved the club and the spear more than they loved their families.

And if the Hill Spirits didn't smile on us now, they'd make war against us soon.

The trail took us up a gentle slope and to a large plateau. There at the center, the Mother's Heart—the Elephant's Heart—waited. Bug Eyes fell to his knees. A pair of rattles appeared in his hands, and he waved them about, making gentle clicking and shaking noises as the other Narrow Ones bowed. Even Star did, though her people had other gods. Why was she doing it? To show respect. I followed her example.

"We give our thanks to the Elephant Mother, who brought life from her womb." He swirled around the procession. Even the Tooth King had bowed his head. "All things are her children. The tiger in the cave. The deer in the forest. The bird in the sky and the fish in the river. She birthed them all, and for this, we thank her—for the gift of life."

"The gift of life!" Everyone repeated it.

Strange stories. A mammoth mother birthing all life? How could that be?

But this place was still sacred. The Hill Spirits had built what the Thin Ones called the Mother's Heart, and generations of hunters had added to it. Broadhead as well as Narrow Ones. Now, it stood as a reminder to everyone about the power of the hunt, to honor those that wielded the spear in search of food, and the beasts they killed to feed us. And in this holy place, no blood could be shed.

Perfect for a peaceful meeting.

We went further on and soon came to the shrine itself. It stood on an expanse of stone at the center of the plateau—countless mammoth tusks jutting up in endless, spiraling rows. Some tusks looked as old as the stones they sat on: splintered, yellowed, and fallen from their perches. Others had been placed recently, the ivory bright. Some had been carved, some with strings of colored rock, teeth, twigs, or other offerings set amongst them. Others just stood bare, their curling tips jabbing upwards to the sky.

A holy place of tusks, shining in the sunlight. My breath slowed as I gazed upon it. Like walking into the home of the Spirits.

We had not arrived first. The Broadheads had set up a little camp at a respectful distance from the holy circle of tusks. They had a few hide tents and a couple fires to keep away the cold and to roast their meat. The Hill People, their furs covered in the gray dust of their homes—as familiar to me as the air we breathed—stood as we approached, many reaching for their spears and clubs. Just being cautious. No war yet.

Song and Rock sat together near the fire, and they both hoisted their hands in greeting.

Across from them, the Frost Clan had made their camp. They wore the furs of white wolves and cave bears, stained with blue dye in wild patterns, with pale ivory piercings on their ears and noses. They raised shrill voices in excited shrieks and squeals, pointing at our arrival—but most were focused on a wrestling match, going on in the center of their encampment.

It was White Hair, fighting one Hill and two Frost warriors.

And winning.

She had the Hillman locked in her arms, holding him in place. Muscle bulged under her cloak—the fur of a white saber-tooth tiger. Tattoos—something the Frost Clan had learned from their trade with the Heap—shone in curling blue lines across her thick, pale arms. She had a mane of white hair, wild and coursing over her shoulders, her face in an expression of fierce joy as she choked the Hillman until his arms flailed. Then she dropped him.

The two Frost Men ran at her, screeching. She sidestepped one and slammed an elbow into his face, then grabbed his head, spun him around, and shoved him into the other. They fell down in a tangle, and she pelted them with kicks from her bare feet, letting out a panting laugh with each blow. Soon, they rolled over and showed their hands.

She'd won.

"You're slow!" She spoke in the speech of the mountains—I could understand it well enough, though some words sounded a little different. "Slow, slow, slow!" She clapped her hands. "Go and walk away. You were good. But I am better." Then she looked up. Noticing us for the first time.

White Hair walked past her warriors, pausing to reach down and grab a two-handed club of white wood and stone. Other Frost Men fell into step behind her. She gave no order, but they were like a pack of wolves following the lead animal: they just knew. Then she hopped onto a rocky outcropping to look down at us.

Despite myself, my hand tightened around my spear.

Then she dropped him.

"These are the Heap's people. The Thin Ones who want our new hunting grounds." She put her hands on her hips. "They look very strange."

"Protect the King!" Purple Plume gave the order. The Feathers moved in front of the litter, forming a line and clutching their spears. The Broadhead warriors readied their own spears, the Hill Clan, led by Song and Rock, hastened to join them. Star slid closer to me, a hand going to the lance on her back.

My breath froze. A harsh word, a slip on the cold stone—a jab in the air with the spear. Any of that could start a fight. My own spear was in my hand.

Would the war start here? And what side would I be on?

The Tooth King held up both hands. "Purple Plume—I know you will always defend me. But we are here to talk peace. Do not show your weapons to those who would be our friends." He spoke it louder. "Away with them—I command it." Plume glanced from the King to his men, and nodded. They brought up their spears and stood at the ready. "Red." The Tooth King pointed to me. "Speak to them in the language of Broadheads. Put flowers around your words. Tell them we only want to talk."

White Hair smiled suddenly, showing the gaps in her teeth. She repeated his words—in the way that Thin Ones talked. "Only want to talk. Good. We talk." How did she know the words of the Heap? She clapped her hands and bellowed commands to the Frost People. They hastened away, dragging the beaten combatants with them and forming a crowd clustered closer to the ruins. White Hair walked to her camp and grabbed a bear fur carpet. She unrolled it herself and settled down, then patted the dark fur next to her. "Come, big Tooth King." She smiled as she talked in the speech of the Heap. "We talk."

The Tooth King clapped his hands and his slaves lowered the litter. He emerged and approached, but remained on his feet—which made him bigger than White Hair. "You speak our language. That is interesting to me." The rest of the Heap Men stood ready—the Feathers still gripping their spears. Bug Eyes shook his rattles and Star looked ready to fight. Good Wolf sensed it too, and her ears tented.

"I learn Thin One words." White Hair reached back and grabbed a bowl of boar jerky. She chewed as she talked. Like she and the Tooth King were just two friends sharing some meal in the Cook's Cave. "Thin Ones come to mountains. Sometimes, we make them stay. They teach me." She chewed hungrily. "You want our food?"

"I still want Red with me. Just to help." He motioned to me.

I hastened to his side, furred boots brushing over the stone. I pointed to Good Wolf. "Stay." She sat down, close to Star, Autumn, and Bug Eyes, and stayed.

We stood together, looking at White Hair—a quizzical look in the Tooth King's eyes. He was wondering if he should take the food. Was this the first time I had ever seen him confused? I nodded. When a host offered a guest food, they had to accept. That was one of the greatest rules of the Hill Spirits. Narrow One Gods taught respect for guests too. The Tooth King had to know that.

Maybe, he was just surprised that Broadheads were good to guests as well.

"I would be honored to accept." He took a chunk of the meat from her hands and set it in his mouth. The chewing took effort, and he forced away a grimace as he worked it in his teeth—before swallowing it down. "And I have gifts for you as well."

Two slaves came up bearing an elegantly carved spear, a scepter tipped with shining stones, and a beautiful woven scarf of bright fox fur. They set them down in front of White Hair. Each gift alone would cost fistfuls of teeth.

She picked up the spear. "Look at this twig." Speaking in Broadhead words. "If you stabbed a rhino with it, the rhino would laugh." She pointed to me. "You—you're Red. You were a Hillman. Now you're with the Heap." She patted the gifts. "You know the ways of the Heap. Tell me, what is their purpose?"

I shrugged. What was their purpose? What would Star say? "They are good—good to the eye. They make the heart happy to see."

"Hmmm." White Hair switched back to the Heap's words. "Thank you."

The Tooth King bowed his head, ever so slightly. It was a strange thing. "And I thank you, for coming here and agreeing to meet. We can talk together. We can find a solution to the problem of the Flowering Fields."

A harsh grunt. "Problem? There is no problem. The Fields are now the Frost People's hunting grounds. If we see Thin Noses there, we kill them. Stay away from the Fields—there will be no problem."

The Tooth King's face remained impassive. "That's not how it will be."

"No?" She took another bite of jerky. "Thin One bones are twigs. I break them—like that." She snapped a finger. "Our warriors kill yours. Maybe we lose a few. But we win. If you don't want to die, stay away from the Fields. Now that you know, you will stay away. There will be peace." She swallowed. "My talk is done."

He sighed and looked at me. "She should hear it in her own language. Tell her how the Heap will make war."

I knew about the way the Heap fought. When the Bull Islanders settled further up the Blood River and tried to take over our fishing routes, they'd gone to war. I had just arrived in the Heap, and saw the results.

I needed to tell White Hair what I had seen. "It will not be like when Broadheads fight—when warriors meet and several on each side die. Or when one clan raids another, and kills several, and steals what they can before leaving." I crouched down so I could look White Hair in the eyes. "Thin Ones have a different kind of war. They strike with arrows from a distance. They plan—they set traps. They will strike where you do not expect, in great numbers. Ten and ten and ten more, fighting as one. They will kill everyone— they won't stop until all your warriors are dead. Then they will go into your caves and burn what they cannot take. If anyone survives, they'll be taken and made into *slaves*." This was a word the Broadheads didn't have. "They'll be used like tools. And serve the Heap."

"No Frost People will serve the Heap!" She roared the words.

"The children will," I said. "Because everyone else will be dead."

She fell silent and looked at the Tooth King. His face stayed impassive— trusting that my threat had done its job.

"But it doesn't have to be that way." I clasped my hands. "I call upon the Hill Spirits. Let them prove to you that I speak truth. You can share the Flowering Fields. There can be peace. Nobody has to die."

Except the vision the Blood-Spiller had given me came back. Broadhead bones littering the floor of our caves. The end of my people.

"Come to the Heap." The Tooth King spoke gently. "There, I have maps, and scribes to record our decisions." She squinted in confusion. "Pictures to draw. Of the land." More confusion. "Never mind—you will see. But there, in my cave, with all the comforts you desire, we will talk until we find a solution to this problem. A way to share, so that we are both happy." He offered his hand. "Let there be no war at all."

She looked to me. "Does he speak truth?"

I nodded. "By the Hill Spirits, I swear he does. Go and be his guest."

"What if it's a trap? Thin Noses are cunning. They are good at setting traps."

I turned to the Tooth King. "She fears a trap."

"Bring your warriors with you. All of them. Let them bring their weapons. I promise you, there will be no trap."

She thought for a moment, cupping her chin. Then she smiled and nodded her head. "If it is a trap, we will just kill any Thin Ones before they can hurt us. We will go there. But we'll spend the night here. This is a sacred place, built by the Frost Spirits and our hunters have added many tusks in their honor. Tomorrow, we will go to the Heap." She took the Tooth King's hand. "You are an interesting Thin One. I will speak with you more."

He shook. "You are very interesting yourself, White Hair."

"Go back to your warriors, Tooth King." White Hair stood and faced me. "I want to talk to Red."

A quick glance from the Tooth King—a little nod—was he concerned about me? Then he walked back to the litter. The other Heap men, even the Feathers, had relaxed a little, leaning on their spears and huddling in their coats. The Frost Broadheads closed in, joining White Hair. A few took jerky from her bowl and chewed. I was alone, surrounded by the Frost People. Even though I wasn't a Hillman anymore, and there was no war on, a chill prickled my skin— like all of their warriors were made of ice and had cooled the air around me.

Until Star hurried over to join me. Good Wolf trotted over too, and sat on her haunches by my side.

White Hair folded her arms and looked at her and at me. "I heard stories about you, Red. The Broadhead in the Heap. I thought you must be a weakling, but you seem strong."

"What's she saying?" Star asked.

She spoke the words of the Heap. "I thought he was weak. But he is strong."

"He's not weak." A singing voice—Song. He walked over, along with Rock. They both embraced me and hugged me tight. Song nuzzled my forehead. "He had a choice to make and he made it. That's all."

"And listen to this—if you can understand." Star spoke up. "A Night Demon captured him. Just last night. And he fought that monster to a standstill and escaped."

They all stared at each other. Were her words true? Either way, I was glad she said them.

White Hair cocked her head. "I thought wrong about you, Red. You are not weak after all."

Something cold slammed into my cheek. I spun around, raising my spear. Packed ice, a sharp cold—clinging to my beard and pressing to my skin. A snowball. It came from a young Broadhead, perhaps Mouse's age of nine or ten summers, with a mass of hair the color of dark mud and a brilliant smile. He stood on top of a stone outcropping, already reaching down to prepare another snowy attack.

"Muddy!" White Hair hooted. "Get down here!" The boy stuck his tongue out and waved his arms like a bird trying to fly. "Get down here or I'll feed you to the bears!"

That did the job. He scrambled down and hurried to join us, his arms behind his back. His eyes remained on me. "You're Red—you're the one that lives in the Heap. Is it true that the Thin Ones are magical? That they can make pieces of wood and stone fly?" His words died on his lips as he stared at Good Wolf. "And they can talk to animals—this must be one of those!"

"My son, Muddy." White Hair laughed and patted his head. "He makes my heart sing."

Muddy lunged out and pressed his hand against Good Wolf's face—

running his fingers along her muzzle before moving it up to flatten her ears. It was pure stupidity. Star gasped. If Good Wolf snapped, Muddy would lose a finger at best.

I jabbed my hand in front of him—putting it between Good Wolf's jaws and the boy's fingers. Muddy stumbled—and fell on the ground. But Good Wolf only opened her mouth to lick his fingers. Her warm spit clung to him.

He giggled. "I've never felt a wolf's tongue before. I'm going to grab it."

"Don't." I glared at him. If my dog devoured White Hair' son, we would have war right there. I looked at White Hair—she didn't yell at her son or tell him to stop. Would she be angry if I smacked him? Probably best to keep my hands still. "Leave her alone."

He looked at Star. "And what does she have on her back? Can I see it?"

Star deserved to know what he was saying. "He wants the Lance of the Skies," I explained.

Star leaned closer and lowered her voice—so White Hair couldn't hear. "If this white bear cub tries to take the lance, I'll throw him right off this mountain."

"You can't see it," I told Muddy.

"Why not?"

Telling him Star's threat was probably a bad idea. Instead, I decided to lie. "It's made of fire. If you touch it, your hands will catch on fire."

His eyes went wide. "Thin Ones really are magic!"

White Hair laughed. "He likes you, Red—and he likes your wolf too." She reached over and patted me. "You fight Night Demons and speak for the Heap—and you are good with Muddy. The Hill Spirits made you well." She looked at Song and Rock. "I think you made the wrong choice. You would have been better in the hills. Maybe then, I would have fought you in a raid, and it would have been a good fight." She grabbed Muddy's arm. "Come on. You can play with the wolf later." She dragged him further back to their tents.

Song laughed, a musical squeak, before gripping my shoulders and pressing his head against mine. "I miss you, Red. We all miss you. In the hills, you would have ten who love and care for you, and ten again, and again still. But it seems you have ones who love and care for you amongst the Thin Noses."

"What is he saying?" Star asked.

"In the hills, I would have friends. But it seems I have friends in the Heap."

"Hmmm." She pointed over to the Heap people—building our camp for the night. Autumn was there, examining mammoth tusks. Studying them with the same careful eye, the same passion, that she studied everything else. "And more than friends."

I blushed. Song saw it and followed my gaze and let out a whooping whistle.

Rock even grinned—something rare for him. I wanted to throw snowballs at all of them. Instead, I trotted over to join Autumn.

That night, I sat next to Autumn and we watched Bug Eyes pray before the Mother's Heart. He had arranged a strange headdress, a set of antlers projecting from above his bug mask, with feathers and strips of fur placed around his outfit, and he cast strange herbs into the fires arranged around the tusks, causing the flames to flicker and dance and change color—or maybe that was just the moonlight. He grabbed a sort of broom, the twigs burning, and used it to whisk the smoke in curling trails around the tusks. As he did, he danced and hummed.

Meanwhile, the Tooth King had some of his men set out jugs of fruit juice, flowers, and slaughtered rabbits at the bases of the tusks, as offerings to the Elephant Mother. Thanking her for bringing the world from her womb. Bug Eyes waved his smoke over each one, then angled the brush toward the sky, like the Elephant Mother's trunk would reach down from the darkness and grab what she wanted.

Narrow Face Gods—so difficult to please.

Across from him, the priests of the Broadheads gave their thanks. The Hill Clan had a Stone Speaker, who could put his ear to the ground and hear the words of the Hill Spirits, and he sang out a repeating chat. Praising the Hill Spirits for making us from earth and stone.

The Frost Clan had their own shaman, clad in the skin of white reindeer, bears, and wolves, and bearing a great curling staff set with countless shards of ivory. He told a story, mixing the words with sung sections that he chanted in his echoing, warbling voice—adding snatches of birdsong to the tale. The story concerned the first members of the Frost People, who battled their way out of the ice, killed the Gods who had put them there, and fashioned the world of their bones and blood.

The prayers of the three curled together, mixing themselves up. They seemed to echo, and I couldn't tell where one ended and the other began.

But the Song of the Stones—I'd heard it for many seasons. Almost every few days, we would gather around the fire, blinking our eyes from the smoke, and sing. The words had been burned into my brain. I repeated them, whispering them under my breath as the Stone Speaker sang.

Autumn noticed. "You know the words. I guess you would—you must have sung them so many times." She pointed to the Stone Speaker. "What do they mean?"

"He's thanking the Hill Spirits for making us. They built us out of rock and earth and filled us with life. Song thinks they did it as a joke, but we must thank them for giving us life."

"The Elephant Mother birthed us all from her womb," Autumn corrected me carefully. "And the Thunder Serpent coiled around the sun and squeezed until life ran down into the mouths of the first men. That's what Bug Eyes is singing." She hesitated. "Everyone has their own story, it seems. There are similarities, but differences too." Her face scrunched up. I'd seen that before—when she became lost in thought. "They can't all be true—can they?"

"I don't know."

"I don't either."

I laughed—hating the squeal in it. "That seems to be a rare thing."

"Why did you leave them?" she asked. "You seem to still like the Hills. They care for you. That's clear. Why did you leave?"

Should I tell her? No—Star knew, and the Tooth King knew—but that was enough. Her eyes glittered—worry, perhaps. I lay down on the bearskin run Autumn had unrolled and said nothing. Good Wolf took the opportunity to sit and rest her head on my belly. I looked at the stars instead. We stared at the sky together.

The songs of three tribes echoing in our ears.

We left when the sun flashed faint in the distance. Better to be on the road in the early morning, when it was still cold. Let the Eaters sleep in their clearings as we went peacefully by and returned to the Heap. We would be a big target—the procession from the Heap, including the Tooth King, and the Hill Clan and Frost Clan as well. Though, given that White Hair and her warriors walked alongside us, we would not be easy to take.

The journey took most of the day. Muddy had to stop to make water in the trees, and White Hair would bellow and slam her great, two-handed club against the tree trunks or the floor until we stopped and waited for him to go and return before we could continue on the path. Then Muddy would want to follow me, to tug at Good Wolf's tail and throw clumps of ice at my back.

I had an urge to hurl him into the Blood River—but did not do it.

Then, with the sun low, we made it back to the Heap.

It loomed tall, just over the bridge crossing the Blood River, the many fires and torches lighting it up from the distance. Making a mountain glow. The Broadheads stared in silence, many falling to their knees or uttering prayers. Song hurried to me. "This is where you live?" He demanded. "This is home? No—this is the home of spirits. Not men."

"This is home," I told him.

But something was wrong. As we went up the slope winding its way into the Heap, nobody hurried out to greet us. Only a few curious children watched from the ledges and caves. No songs amongst the fires, and while merchants stood by the frog ponds, none called out to us or offered their food in exchange for teeth.

They just watched, stared at the Broadheads in fear, and looked away.

Star noticed it too. "Look—Spinner." She pointed to the top of the slope, and an outcropping where a fire burned. "If anyone knows what's going on, it's her." She tugged my arm. I glanced back at Autumn, who nodded, and then I followed after her.

Tale-Spinner had her usual crew and a large audience—bigger than the one I had seen the night I battled the Blood-Spiller. More puppets danced in the lowlight of the blaze. "And there is Scribbles, the good scribe—see how he goes so willing—so trusting!" A puppet representing Scribbles danced above the fire—composed of twigs ending in burned charcoal sticks. "He follows the Broadhead Fang. Follows him without a care." There was the puppet representing me—the stuffed badger. "Right into the Blood-Spiller's hands." The Blood-Spiller puppet swept down in another storyteller's hands, rushing into the scribe.

That was a lie!

I stormed closer, gripping my spear. "Spinner!" I shouted her name. "You say that I led Scribbles to the Blood-Spiller? That I would hurt him?"

A rustle of whispers around the fire. Everyone pointed at me, whispering. Spinner went to her feet. "You tell me, Red. He went with you, and now you're here and he's with the Rider."

Oh, no. May the Spirits say that wasn't so. But I knew it was. I had known as soon as I woke up in the Blood-Spiller's cave and Scribbles wasn't anywhere to be found.

"What happened?" I asked, as Star hurried over.

"You don't know?" Spinner asked.

"What happened!?" My voice rose to a screech.

Spinner looked back at her audience. "They found Scribbles this morning. By the river. With dirt and a seed in his mouth."

I stabbed my spear into the fire, striking the burning wood and sending up a spew of ash and sparks. "Red—careful!" Star grabbed my arm. "I know—there is fire in your heart. Calm it."

I stopped. Every Thin Nose pair of eyes around the fire watched me—fearfully.

"Can we trust the Broadhead?" Spinner said the words that all had to be thinking. "And now, there's more of them." She pointed to the causeway, where the Frost Clan and the Hill Clan headed up, still staring around in amazement. "There is savagery in their hearts, after all. The Blood-Spiller wears a mask. Who's to say his brows aren't big and his nose thick?"

That wasn't true. I had seen the Blood-Spiller, and he was clearly a Thin Nose. But these people didn't know that. They were already scared of Broadheads, and this was another scary story, with the monster—or monsters—now very close by.

Star picked up a clay jug full of water. "Story time is over." She upended it, right into the fire. "Go back to your caves."

Smoke burst over the audience, making a chorus of coughs.

"You can't—" Spinner started.

Star fixed her with a glare that stabbed like a spear—harsh enough to stop any argument, and then patted my shoulder. "Come on, Red. We have more to do."

She was right. We followed the procession of Broadheads making their way to the top of the Heap.

CHAPTER FIVE
THE FLOOD OF BLOOD

The next day, soon as the sun cut through the mist, one of the stranger meetings in all of the Heap's memory took place in the Tooth King's cave. The Tooth King himself has asked for me to be there, to take words from the tongue of the Frost Clan and make them the words of the Heap. But I was the only Fang there, and feathery drifts of fear danced around my heart. It was like the Hill Spirits had carried me away to one of the wild celebrations they had in the clouds during a storm, and they'd be dancing around lightning fires and drinking from the rain while I watched.

But I went despite my fear. It was the task of the Fang. And it might stop war.

I sat on a stone covered in leopard skin blankets, the Tooth King next to me on his throne. He had a few of his Feathers with him, including Purple Plume.

They rested their spears on their shoulders and gazed at the Broadhead guests like hunters who expected a cornered tiger to leap out and start biting. Across from them sat White Hair and ten of her best warriors, along with Rock and Song—the other Hillmen waiting in the tent outside.

White Hair and the Frost People men treated it like a giant party. The Tooth King had ordered a massive feast prepared, and Cook in the Cook Cave and all his slaves and kin produced enough food to make a cave bear happy. They had boar ribs arranged in elegant pyramids, great bowls of berries of different colors, fermented and pulped fruit stabbed through straws, fish steaming with eyes staring at everything in confusion. All draped in sweet and spicy herbs that made the Heap's food tastier than anything I ate in the hills, and laid out on neat blankets and reed mats on the floor of the cave.

"By the cold winds and the ancient frost, by the giants of sky and stone—this is good!" White Hair leapt at the feast before the Tooth King could stop her. "Come on, friends!" She beckoned as she handed Muddy—the little Broadhead had come with her, unfortunately—a fistful of ribs. "Eat!"

They attacked the feast with pure ferocity. Broadheads were big eaters, and watching big eaters eat big food was not exactly pretty. White Hair scooped up the fish first and devoured it from the head on down—sucking up the eyes before ripping at the delicate, pale flesh. The smaller bones she crunched loudly, the bigger were spat out, and the Tooth King's new cats fought over them in hissing battles. Other Broadheads hoisted meat above their heads and slurped at the juices trickling down or scooped up fistfuls of berries and jammed them into their mouths. Muddy grabbed a slice of roasted root and tossed it at me.

The Tooth King watched them and said nothing.

"Like animals," Purple Plume muttered.

"Put flowers around your words when you speak about our guests." The Tooth King glared at Purple Plume before raising his voice. "White Hair! Do you find the food delicious?" He nudged me, and I did my best to translate.

"He asks if you think the food good?" I asked.

She spoke in the Heap tongue. "Good, good, good!" Meat juice drizzled over her chin and she wiped it with her fingers—then licked the fingers. "This is a place of wonders." She pointed to the cats. "Look at those—and those!" She nodded toward the cave hyenas, who had curled up in the corner of their pen. "I can see why you want to stay here, Red. If we raid this place, we'll have to take some of this goodness back."

"You shouldn't raid them," Rock said. "Remember what Red said about how they make war. Make peace with them—or many will die."

"Us and them," Song sang. "Make peace, White Hair, and there will be peace."

Her smile faded and her face went serious. Odd next to all the grease stains. She hadn't forgotten why she was here. "Tooth King." She switched to the Heap tongue. "Peace—you want peace. The Frost People wants peace too. But we want the Flowering Fields to hunt and you want them—you want them for something else."

"I know," the Tooth King said. "What should we do? I have a way to solve the problem."

He motioned to the wall. A stoop-shouldered slave pulled away a cave lion skin blanket, revealing an intricate painting—a sort of lumpy shape. I squinted at it, and the bright colors. Brilliant hues of green, a swirling band of blue. Green puffs, marked with red dots like wounds from a bone needle. More pricks of brilliant color, scattered about the green. What was this? Some sort of Night Demon, with a misshapen body and more eyes than I could count?

White Hair looked similarly confused. "What is this?"

"These are the Flowering Fields." The Tooth King spoke slowly, pointing with his thick figure. "You see? Those are the trees. Those are the flowers, and the river. The whole meadow is here. It is a Place Drawing."

"Wrong." White Hair walked closer and stared at the painting. "The Flowering Fields look different." She switched to Broadhead speech. "Why have they done this, Red? This is like no drawing I've ever seen. Is the Tooth King touched by the Hill Spirits?"

"Imagine you're a bird." The Tooth King stretched out his hands. "You are flying and looking down. This is what you would see—a Place Drawing." He sighed. "Look, do you see the stones in the middle?" He pointed to a few splotches of gray. "That's the midway point. The Moon Pools. The middle of the Flowering Fields. You will get the north, for your hunting and we'll get the south. We'll have trees there, growing—and you must not take our apples."

"*Your* apples?" White Hair stared at me. "This is pure foolishness. Apples have no owner. Did they carve the apples? Did they sew the apples? How can the apples be theirs? If I want to take an apple and eat it, that is what I do. Why should these apples be any different?"

I would have to explain. In the way of Broadheads. A difficult task, especially because I didn't understand Autumn's plans myself.

"They'll grow the apples themselves. Along with other plants." I tried my best to tell White Hair the truth. "They'll plant the seeds. Bring in the water. Put them in the sunlight. Keep away pests. And then the plants will be theirs."

"The plants will be theirs…" White Hair repeated the words. "Why would they do that? There are animals to hunt. There are berries and roots to gather. Why work so hard for something that will grow anyway?"

The Tooth King stared at me, attentive—waiting for our conversation in

Broadhead Speech to end. Knowing that I was loyal to him. That I would say the words that made White Hair agree to his plan.

But I thought about what the Blood-Spiller had said. "There will be more of them—much more food, so their tribe can grow. They'll grow and grow." And spread across the face of the earth like a swarm of locusts. Wiping away the Broadheads.

Leaving only our bones behind, lost and dusty in distant caves. Just like in the vision the Blood-Spiller had given me.

Part of me wanted to say that, to urge White Hair not to agree. To promise war.

But the words didn't leave my mouth. I stayed silent.

White Hair shrugged and switched back to the tongue of the Heap. "So, you get half. We get half. That's what you want?"

"Yes!" The Tooth King clasped his hands. "Exactly!"

"What about them?" White Hair pointed to Rock and Song. "How much will the Hill People get?"

"They'll share your half." The King pointed again to the Place Drawing. "Half for the Heap. Half for Broadheads."

"You think Hill and Frost are the same?" Rock spoke up now, coming to his feet and holding his spear in both hands. Either he didn't realize that the Tooth King couldn't understand him, or he didn't care. "We have warred, ten times and ten times again. They have raided us, and slain many, and we have met their warriors and killed them. If you think we will share, that we'll hunt with them—" He tapped his spear butt against the stone floor, letting all hear the clicks. "Then there will be war. I swear by the stones!"

The Tooth King leaned closer to me. "Calm your kinsman down."

What was I to say? What could take the fire from his heart? "Rock, there is friendship here. Do not bring anger to the Tooth King's cave."

"I'll bring anger where I want." He pointed to me. "You're of the hills, Red—but you're also not. You're with the Heap now."

Song stepped closer to his mate. "Cruel words. No need for them." He hummed as he sniffed Rock, and nuzzled him—smoothing down his hair and planting a kiss on his cheek. "Remember why we're here. We want peace. They want peace. Even the Frost Men want peace. We just have to talk—and we'll have peace."

"Peace." Rock repeated. "Yes—tell the Tooth King that, Red. We don't war. But we need our hunting too."

"What does the Tooth King say to that?" White Hair asked.

I faced the Tooth King. "Hill Clan and Frost Clan. They are not the same. You can't put the Flowering Fields into two pieces, give them half, and expect them to share."

The Tooth King brushed his hand over his plump cheeks, wiggling the crystal studs worked into his skin. "May the Elephant Mother grant me patience. May the Monkey Boy grant me wisdom." He looked back at the map. "What if there were different times? The Hill gets the summer and the Frost get the spring? Or what if we left them part of the plants that we take from the trees? Maybe that will—"

But a yelp from Muddy interrupted the thoughts he put into words. We all spun around. The Broadhead boy had scrambled over the bone fence and joined the two cave hyenas in their pen. He had leapt onto the back of one cave hyena, digging his hands into the fur, and holding on tightly. The hyena released a panicked, trilling giggle and dashed around the pen, its friend scampering along close behind.

If that boy got bitten by the cave hyenas, White Hair might go to war with the Heap right then and there.

I was closest to the pen. I leapt inside, crossing the fence as Muddy rode the hyena in a panicked, looping circle—right next to me. My hand jabbed out and I grabbed Muddy by the back of his white reindeer fur vest. He squeaked as I pulled him free. The hyena kept going, spun around and joined its fellow. They both snarled at me, their high-pitched laughs echoing through the caves as they flashed teeth.

Remember Good Wolf. Would what worked on her work on these? I had to try.

I held out both hands and shouted, roaring as loud as I could—making myself as big as I could. The cave hyenas laughed back at me, but stayed put.

Then the Tooth King grabbed some boar ribs from the feast and threw one to each of his pets. The hyenas fell on them, tearing at the meat before snapping with their big jaws. I tucked Muddy under my arm, crossed the pen, and plopped him down.

He had sunshine in his smile. "Did you see that, my mother?" He grinned at White Hair. "The hyena carried me!"

White Hair laughed. "You two were like a shooting star across the night sky!"

The Tooth King stared at me and cleared his throat. "Perhaps it would be good if the young one was not here." I agreed. He pointed to me. "Red, you should take young Muddy to see the Heap. Show the boy all of the miracles that we have made here." That, I didn't like at all. "And keep him safe."

I tried to think of a reason why I couldn't take him. "You need someone to make the Heap's words into Broadhead words."

"White Hair speaks enough of the Heap's tongue. And there are others who have learned the speech of Broadheads." The Tooth King nodded toward the cave entrance. "Take a bag of teeth. Buy him whatever he wants—keep him happy."

White Hair held out her hand and Muddy scurried to join her. "What are you talking about?" She patted his head, nearly knocking him down with her heavy hand.

"They want me to take Muddy to the Heap—so you and the Tooth King can talk." Please, in the name of the Hill Spirits, refuse. "But if don't want—"

She faced her son. "What do you say, Muddy?"

He jumped up and down, his body shaking with joy. "I want to go with Red!"

Well, there was nothing more to be said. He was the son of White Hair and the son of White Hair got what he wanted. I snorted and balled my hands into fists. Now, I'd have to make sure Muddy wasn't hurt, that he was happy, and that I didn't throw him off the Heap or feed him to any hungry animals.

I'd had an easier time with the mammoths.

I decided the Trader's Ledge was the perfect place to take him. When I had first come to the Heap, I had spent many moments here, seated on a rock and watching the people of the Heap at their tents, offering their goods for barter or teeth. Hunters sold horn and hide, gatherers brought flowers in countless hues and berries for eating and painting, and there was always music or Spinner or one of her fellow storytellers in a cluttered corner. For the young, there were toys—soft, lumpy creatures of stuffed deer hide or carved figurines of horn and ivory. They even had a little sling, a toy and not a weapon, of leather hide, that could send a pebble or a berry whistling toward a target.

Muddy wanted one, and whined until I plopped down the teeth to buy it and more for a pouch of stinky berries. "I give you gratitude!" He put a berry in the sling and started swinging it over and over—trying to get a feel for an object unknown in the mountains.

I caught his wrist before he could send a berry flying. "What do you want now?"

"Food—I am hungry." He rubbed his stomach and smiled.

"You just ate. The feast the Tooth King provided."

"But I'm hungry now!"

I grunted. The Cook Cave was close by, at least. I led him over and went

"I want to go with Red!"

to the cave in the corner of the Ledge, where Cook worked to make some of the tastiest meats that had ever touched a tongue. There was Cook, moving between a set of pits where fire flickered over different sorts of meat, pausing to add a spray of spices from the pouches and pockets of his coat, or lean down and run his tongue along a particular chunk. I held up two fingers and set a few teeth down on the flat stone near the entrance of his cave. He drew a sharp stone knife, sliced carefully, and soon, Muddy and I each had a chunk of spiced aurochs' belly with some roasted roots on the side.

We settled down at the corner of the market and gnawed on the meat. A little band worked at flutes and drums, gathering a crowd. For a few moments, Muddy filled his mouth with food and not with words. Thank the Hill Spirits.

Then he pointed to the edge of the market. "Look—more youngsters!"

It was a cluster of orphans. Mother Rat's children. They came dancing out amongst the crowd, a ragged pack. They worked like a pack too—one making a feint toward a wrinkled woman selling gathered apples to distract her, while another swept in and carefully snatched away a fruit. Mother Rat trained them, like any mother did her children, and they had learned their ways well. I could go over to them, force the rat children to return the apple, and deal out a few kicks as punishment. But I had Muddy to watch.

And there were bigger problems to worry about.

Mouse split away from the group and scampered over to join us. She folded her legs and sat next to us, her eyes instantly going to the slices of glazed belly, the charred herbs curled up against the meat. A true feast for one of Mother Rat's children. Then she looked at Muddy. "Who's he?"

"Muddy." I said his name in Broadhead speech and then the words of the Heap. "And Muddy, this is Mouse."

"Mouse." He grinned at her. "Hello, Mouse! Catch!" Then gave his sling a whirl. One of the little berries flew out and bopped against Mouse's shirt. Oh, why couldn't a Hill Spirit see Muddy and turn him to stone? Or carry him away into the clouds? Mouse squawked and stumbled, before reaching down and grabbed a rock. Muddy's smile faded.

When Mother Rat's orphans played, they played rough.

I moved to stop her. If White Hair's beloved son got pelted with a rock, she'd burn the Heap down. Or at least, that's what I thought would happen.

But Muddy had already held a chunk of meat toward her. "Does your stomach rumble? Is your belly empty?" She couldn't understand his words, but offered food was meaning enough.

Mouse paused, the stone frozen in her fist.

"Hungry—" I told Muddy the Heap word.

"Hungry?" He set the meat down in front of her.

In a second, Mouse had grabbed the meat and gnawed at it. She tore the meat between her sharp little teeth and gobbled it down. Muddy handed her another, for when she had finished.

It was strange, to see a bit of kindness from the boy. But then again, all his foolishness was just how the young acted. I had been like that too, perhaps—or worse. And there was kindness too. I saw it now. Muddy pointed to the meat. "Flesh strips," he explained in Broadhead speech. "Strips of flesh?" Then he pointed to Mouse.

She had grease over her chin and wiped it on her arm. "Roasted aurochs belly," she said—using the Heap words.

Well, if they could get along, maybe there was hope for the rest of us. Provided the Tooth King and White Hair negotiated right.

"Red!" Star's voice. She came walking through the cold market, her hide boots crunching in the snow. A bit of frost had settled on her mammoth cloak. She stared from me to Muddy. "You are playing father to the Broadhead boy?" Right now, Muddy and Mouse were saying words wrong—and giggling at the garbled phrases in each of their tongues.

I grunted. "You think I could be a father?"

"You take care of your dogs, don't you?" She lowered her voice. "I come from the Cave of the Gods. Bug Eyes prepared Scribbles' body for burial. His family was there—making offerings by the Rider for a safe journey."

They would have been weeping, and not alone in their tears. I was glad I hadn't gone with them. "What did Bug Eyes find?"

"The same as Frog Face. Dirt in the mouth. The same seed within. The Wrong Death came from the strike of a blade, sharp and cruel, between the ribs. Slicing hard to the side." When had the Blood-Spiller done it? I must have been lost in dreams, tied up in his hut—useless as a dead man—while that Night Demon slaughtered Scribbles. Star touched my hand. "It happened fast. There was nothing you could have done."

I looked away, staring at the meat in front of me. The good, spicy tang faded—it tasted bad now. "Found in the river, like Frog Face."

"Much further upstream. Closer to Eater Territory." She tapped the table. "That worries me. How does he move so fast?"

"He's a Night Demon."

She spat on the snow at her feet. "He's a man. We'll prove that when we catch him. But something else worries me. Scribbles, Frog Face—they work for this scheme of the Tooth King. To make plants grow." What the Blood-Spiller hated. What he had told me. "The Tooth King and Gummy were behind it, but you might as well try and stab the sun as give the Wrong Death to the Tooth King. And Gummy? He has Raven watching him, like a mother bear watches her cubs." Her voice softened. "But there's someone else involved. Who might be easier to hunt."

"Autumn." I knew it—I should have known it sooner.

She was the one who had created the idea of planting seeds—of growing and then plucking the fruit. Of raising plants like we raised our children. If she was gone, the dream of growing food would fail.

And she was alone, and vulnerable.

I sprang up from the table. "Where is she now?"

"By the stream, near the huts of the fisherwomen." Star spoke fast as Muddy and Mouse fell silent and stared at me—alarmed by the shout in my voice, the fire in my words. "Gathering reeds for her baskets. There are fisherwomen close by. The Blood-Spiller wouldn't try—"

"He would do anything to stop the growing." I picked up my spear and checked my club. It wouldn't take long to reach the Blood River—if we ran. "Muddy, we're going down to the river. I have to see a friend."

A friend—but she was more than that. Thinking of Autumn in danger, Autumn under the Blood-Spiller's blade, put venom in my heart.

"I don't want to go." Muddy shrugged. "I like being here—with Mouse." He said her name, drawing out the middle and wiggling his tongue while did it—making her laugh.

"We leave now!" I screeched at Muddy. He flinched.

A child, after all. And scared when an elder raised his voice. Just like I had been afraid of my father. I paused. It was not his fault that the Blood-Spiller was about. Or that Autumn was in danger.

Mouse perked up. "Are you going? Could I go with you?"

"Why not?" Star asked. "We'll all visit the river."

Like it would be enjoyable. A walk in the sunshine, instead of the falling snow, and the Blood River making a joyful noise as it rushed over the stones. But ice gripped my heart instead as I hurried down, moving at a run that left Star and Mouse and Muddy behind. Because the Blood-Spiller was still out there, and I knew him, and what he would do to Autumn. Maybe this is how my father felt, when I left the hills and went to the Heap.

But this was different. I would do something about it.

We reached the river and the sun sat high, burning away the clouds and making the air clear. A last gasp of warmth and sunshine before winter hit hard. The fisherwomen were still there, setting out their poles and readying their spears to try and catch what they could amongst chunks of ice and snow floating their way along the Blood River. Snow crunched under my boots as I ran down and searched their huts and the trees. No sign of Autumn.

Were we too late?

Star hurried over next, followed by the children. She spoke quickly to a short fisherwoman gutting a trout on a flat stone. "This way—Autumn went downstream." She led the way, moving alongside the riverbank. Mouse and Muddy hurried after us, still chattering in each other's tongue—but they had realized something was wrong. They laughed less and stood close together as they passed under boughs thick with snow.

The Blood River reached a bend, a spit of land jutting out into a mass of reeds. There was Autumn. She knelt beside the river, her little knife slicing at the bases of reeds, chopping them apart, and leaving them in a neat pile by her legs. She stood when we approached, her freckled face splitting into a wide smile.

"Red! And Star—oh, is that Muddy?" She gave him a wave, which he returned. "And who's that with you? One of Mother Rat's?"

"Mouse." Mouse went shy—very odd for her—and looked at deer-hide shoes.

"You and Muddy go play by the river." I walked closer to Autumn. "We have to talk."

Muddy tapped Mouse's arm, let out a yip, and hurried further down the stream—running toward the groves of trees right near the Blood River's edges. Mouse shouted back and dashed after him, already reaching down for a fistful of snow. I hope she sent one whistling right into his face.

Autumn's smile faded. "What's happening?"

"The Blood-Spiller." I walked over to her. Put my hands on her shoulders while Star stood by. "He wants the plants to stop growing."

"Why would he want that?" Autumn shrugged. "Well, it doesn't matter. He can want whatever he wants. He gives the Wrong Death and lurks in the darkness. I don't care what some cave lion or tiger down in the dark places thinks and I don't care what he thinks."

"He's attacking those close to your idea, Autumn." Star counted on her fingers. "Frog Face. Scribbles. And we think he's going to come for you."

Autumn swallowed. "Oh." She drew away from me and clasped her hands. "Two good people. Two of my friends. I think I knew that it would happen— that the Blood-Spiller would come for me. But I didn't want to say it." She stomped a foot down. "But I won't stop. I won't be afraid. He's hurt my friends, and he won't make me stop."

"You should stay in the Heap," I said. "Forget your seeds. Stay in one of the big caves, with everyone. Keep away from the wild places. Never be alone."

"For how long?"

"Until the Blood-Spiller is caught."

"And how long will that take, Red?" She folded her arms, looking as annoyed as Muddy did when I told him we had to go. "Should I stay in a cave for a day? A season? A winter, summer, spring, and—and autumn? Until the Blood-Spiller gets old, sick, and the Rider comes for him as well?"

I didn't have the answer. We hadn't caught the Blood-Spiller—hadn't caught him yet, as he gave the Wrong Death to two people in the Heap. The Fangs were the Tooth King's law, the keepers of his will and the defenders of the Heap. And we couldn't stop him. We hadn't even come close.

Maybe that's what hurt the most.

"You must be safe." It sounded foolish. I said it anyway. "I want you to be safe."

"You think I should do that? To risk everything? Give up on the future? For my sake?" She pointed to me. "Would you ever do something like that?"

I would—and I had. I flinched at the words.

"Autumn." Star stepped closer to me. "You put fire in your words. You need to stop—"

"No." Autumn brushed her past and glared at me. "Tell me, Red. Would you do something like that?"

"It's why I'm here." I glared back. The words spilled out of me now, warm against my tongue. A cut in my mouth, filling it with blood. "A bear hunt in the mountains. A cave bear. My father and I and my village's best hunters. We put smoke into the cave and drove the bear out—and I ran. In my running, I dropped." I rested a hand on my leg. "And what was inside my leg broke during the fall. So that I could not walk without limping."

"You don't limp now—"

In truth, there was a drag in my foot still, and it hurt like now, when the air grew cold—a shard of soreness, stretching below my knee and running to my ankle. "The Broadheads care for our old and sick. We keep them in the caves and warm them and bring them food. But they eat, and cannot hunt or gather—and so they could make a whole tribe die." I patted my leg. "So I made the right choice. I left the hills and wandered down, into the woods."

"To die?"

"I thought I would. I could see the Hill Spirits, dancing around the corners of my vision. Coming to take me. But it was the Tooth King's men instead. They brought me to the Heap, and healed me—and now I cannot go back."

Because once you left the Hills, as I had done, you could not return. The others hunters would not rely on you. They could be friendly toward you. They could embrace you and nuzzle you.

But they could never trust you.

"You risked your life, for the good of your people. For something bigger than you." Autumn took my hand. "It's what a Thin Nose would do. You don't wish to a burden—and still you only think of yourself."

"What do you mean?"

"Do you think your friends would have minded taking care of you for those days? The two who I met—Song and Rock, that's what they're called—they would have fed you and cared for your leg until it healed. Your father too, perhaps. Though I don't know him. But they would have done it. My heart is solid as stone on that. But you didn't give them the chance, because you can be just as selfish as a Thin One—and that's what you're being now."

I didn't know what to say. I hummed instead, and drew her closer to me, and wrapped her in my arms—like those could protect her from the Blood-Spiller.

Then a scream came from further up the riverbank. Mouse's voice.

The young ones. We hadn't been watching them.

Star grabbed her spear and dashed along the reeds. I followed. Autumn came close behind, and that was good. I wanted her close. We splashed along water, swollen from the melting snow, and spilling out of the banks, and there was Mouse.

Lying on the grass, clutching her head. Blood in her fingers.

Star reached her first. She knelt down and gently rolled Mouse over. She brushed back Mouse's hair. "Skin's barely broken—just a bruise." The girl looked like one of the toys that Thin Ones made for their children—a little creation of sewn hide and hair, limp and without life. But Mouse breathed now, coughing, and her eyes fluttered open.

"The Broadhead—Muddy—" She murmured the boy's name.

Where was he? I dashed through the reeds, pushing them aside with my spear. Cold water splashed against my boots, the freeze stinging. I didn't care and pushed on, going further into the reeds and to the river itself. Nothing but the cold river and stones, and silence.

Autumn had joined Star. She used the waterskin at her hip to give Mouse some water, then cleaned the blood from her hair. I looked back and our eyes met. She had all the fear that I felt there, etched into her face.

"What happened?" Star asked.

"A nightmare—a monster." Mouse stood now, still keeping a hand on her head. "He came out of the shadows. The Broadhead boy. He attacked him. Jumped and bit. I tried to help too." She shuddered. "And he hit me and I fell."

We all knew who had done it. There was no doubt who had appeared somehow, moving with impossible speed along the river, and crept like a Night Demon in the stories to attack two young innocents.

But Star asked anyway. "What did he look like?"

"A skull."

No doubt now. It was the Blood-Spiller. He had wanted to kill the future, to stop seeds from growing. So why wouldn't he take someone young, fill his mouth with dirt and a seed, and end any chance of peace?

It would be the biggest Wrong Death of them all.

No chance of tracking him. No chance of finding footprints in the snow—Star located a few, but they vanished at the river's edge. Nothing to do but run back, up into the Heap, and go straight back to the Tooth King's Cave, to tell him what happened. To tell White Hair that her son was in the claws of a Night Demon. We left Autumn with Mouse outside, so that my friend could look over the girl and make certain she had her health.

And I didn't want Autumn or Mouse to see what happened.

After I told White Hair what had happened—in Broadhead speech—she stayed quiet for a moment. Then she reared up with a roar, like she had turned into the bear whose skins made up her cloak and mantle. She grabbed free her giant two-handed club and slammed it into a delicate pot, sending fragments spinning through the air. Fruit juice spilled out. The Tooth King's cats scampered away, hissing in terror.

Then White Hair sprang closer to the Tooth King, her body shaking, her muscles taut. The Feathers darted in front of him, trying to protect the King with their spears—until he held up his hand.

"White Hair. I am sorry." He raised his hands. "We will find him. We will save your son."

"You haven't found this killer yet!" Each word came as a raspy breath, spoken in halting Heap speech. She jabbed her club in my direction. "Who will do it? This one? Who fails?" I'd rather she hit me. I'd rather she put that right in my skull.

"Red was taken unaware. But my Fangs are powerful. I will summon all of them. I will send them into the woods."

"Your Fangs are useless!" She went to me next, club held in both hands, as if readying a swing. "You are not warriors. You are not hunters. You gather nothing. You are the Tooth King's tools. You are tools of the fat and the soft. All you do is hurt the weak. You protect nothing. You save nothing." She slowed, a sudden sob breaking into her words. "You couldn't protect my son."

I clenched my fists and stayed silent. She was right.

"I'll send the Feathers into the forest too." The Tooth King kept up his gentle words. "And our hunters. We have good trackers. We have dogs who can smell a tiger in its den from far away. We will find your son."

"I will be going into the woods too." White Hair started for the door, speaking without looking back at the Tooth King. "I will take all of my warriors." She pointed to Rock and Song and went back to Broadhead speech. "Will the Hillmen go with us? To protect a young one from a monster?"

Rock nodded. Song clasped his hands and sang. "Let Frost and Stone hunt together."

"Good." She turned back to the Tooth King as her warriors walked past her. "And Tooth King—if Muddy is hurt—there will be war." She grunted and strode through the cave mouth, breaking into a run as the path sloped downwards.

The other Broadheads filed after us.

The Tooth King had already started giving orders. "Purple Plume, send a messenger to the other Fangs. We'll go to the borders of Eater Territory. I pray to the Gods that the Blood-Spiller hasn't taken the boy deep into their land." He waved to his slaves. "Make my litter ready. I will go down there as well."

I stepped forward. "Glory to the Tooth King. Should Star and I—"

He cut me off with a wave of his hand. "Star should go. But not you. Go back to your cave."

I lowered my head. A sob slipped out. "I want to be out there."

"Red." The Tooth King waddled closer. He put his hand on my cheek. "You are too close. I need a hunter who can hunt without hate. You hate the Blood-Spiller."

"Does that make me a fool? A weakling?"

"It makes you human." He slipped into Broadhead speech. "A Narrow One." Then he left me and walked toward the mouth of the cave, where slaves waited with his litter. He would oversee the search himself.

While I waited here.

I wandered out after him, Star trailing behind me. She had been quiet during White Hair's rage. Quiet during the Tooth King's commands. When Star got like that, it meant she was thinking. But about what?

Outside, Autumn waited with Mouse. The girl sat on a stone topped with a cushion, looking around in amazement. No orphan ever made it up here. "We saw the Broadheads charge out—then the Tooth King and his men." Autumn looked from me to Star. "They're going into the Bloodwood. To find that poor boy."

"Yes," Star said. "But I think they're wasting their time."

"What do you mean?"

Star stepped near a carved wooden sculpture of a mammoth and rested her hand on the trunk. "We've been thinking about the wrong things. We know why the Blood-Spiller kills. We know, more or less, how he kills. But we don't know who he is. Searching the forest will not work. He won't be found unless he wants to be found. We need to be able to call him out. That means we need to know who he is." She pointed to Autumn. "And I know who would know."

What did she mean? Ask the Hill Spirits, who knew everything?

But Autumn nodded. "Gummy."

"Take us to Gummy's cave. And he will tell us everything he knows about the Blood-Spiller." Star picked up her spear. "And nobody will stop us."

Mouse had been listening carefully. "What should I do?"

"You go see Mother Rat. Tell her what happened." Someone else who might know more—if we forced her to tell the truth. But sending little Mouse to snap at the tail of Mother Rat might not be good. She would need help. "Stop by the cave and pick up Good Wolf for protection. Feed her puppies while you're there. Then go to the Rat's Cave." I rested a hand on Mouse's shoulder. "We will join you and find out the truth." I hesitated. "If you want to."

She brushed back her hair and gazed at me. "Muddy—he is my friend. I'll protect him." Fire in her words.

Just like what burned in my heart.

Autumn took us to Gummy's cave. He didn't even dwell on the Heap itself—but another mountain, a smaller mound of rock close by. I think he wanted the safety that came from living alone. The defense that having so many teeth bought. A wooden rope bridge, the slats set with glittering stones and the ropes of finely woven human hair, deer hide, and mammoth fur, stretching through the cold and reaching its end on his mountaintop. The cold mist and a hint of falling snow around us turned Gummy's home into an island, and the bridge went over a sea.

As we crossed, Star going first and Autumn and I following, I knew why

Gummy had chosen to live in such a place: it made certain that he knew exactly who was coming.

The flap of his cave—a structure built of countless stones set close together—fluttered open. Raven emerged. He walked calmly to the edge of the bridge and waited until we got close. His obsidian-edged weapon rested in his hand, the bottom pointed down. In the dim lights, the stones had lost their shine.

"Why are you here?" Raven asked.

"You heard about what happened, I take it—the Broadhead boy. Taken by the Blood-Spiller." Star spoke quickly.

"You won't find him here." Raven chewed something. He spat it out—sending the pieces flying over the edge and vanishing in the mist. "And Gummy wants no visitors. I don't care what questions you have. Gummy wants you to leave and so you'll leave."

"We won't leave," I replied.

Raven shrugged. A hand slipped into his feather cape. "Yes. That's what I thought you'd say."

Those two round stones, connected by a line of cord—I'd seen them before when he nearly tossed them at me in the Flowering Fields. Now, he sent the stones whistling out, humming as they zoomed through the air. I tried to move back, but the bridge was narrow, and Autumn stood behind me.

The stones went around my legs. They forced them, momentum swinging the points together and tying a knot. He had picked a long rope. They went around even Broadhead legs. The tension stung—like putting my legs into the mouth of a tiger. I tumbled back—falling toward the edge of the bridge. Autumn caught me, grabbing my shoulders as the whole bridge shook and jumped with my weight. My legs slid out over the slats, bound together, and the rest of me nearly followed.

Cold mist below and only Autumn's grip and my back on the slick wooden planks of the bridge to hold me back.

Star ran straight to Raven—taking out the Lance of the Skies. She brought it down, just as he raised his club. Obsidian and the shimmering stone of the heavens crashed together. I caught a glimpse of those strange weapons clashing before I grabbed my spear and spun it around—aiming for the hide cord now tying me up.

"Red—what should I do?" Autumn still held me as I pulled back the spear.

"Don't let me fall." I jabbed out the spear. Sharpened stone stabbed against the cord. It poked, but didn't cut. I kept pushing. More clashes from the mountain. I looked back. Star had forced Raven back with a series of rapid strikes. He blocked them, but she was fast and she was strong. The blows still had to hurt. I needed to get there—to help.

I stabbed out the spear—and nearly sliced into my hide boot and my foot. The cord weakened. I kicked out my legs and it came free. The little stones falling away.

Then I sprang up and ran straight down bridge. Spear leveled—putting speed in the attack.

Raven kicked Star aside. His club came up first, matching my spearpoint. Clicks and sparks. My spear went to the side—but I kept coming. I tackled him. We crashed together on the dirt. One hand settled around Raven's belly. Another rammed against his head—good blow that sent spit flying into the grass.

Something jabbed into my throat.

"Raven!" Autumn cried. "Stop!"

Raven drew back his hand. He had an obsidian dagger there. Above him, Star had the Lance of the Skies pointed at the back of his head.

"Gummy will want to see me, won't he?" Autumn kept talking. "And these are my friends. If he doesn't see them, if he doesn't answer their questions—I'll never plant another seed for him again."

The flap opened again—just a little. "Autumn. My beloved. You wouldn't do that."

"It's not worth it." She shouted back. "Not the lives of my friends. Not the life of that Broadhead boy. I swear by all the Gods, you hurt them, and all the seeds go right into the river. We'll let them get planted that way."

Silence—then a response. "Come in."

Raven rolled over and pushed me off. I glared at him. "I would have beaten you down, if the fight went longer." He said nothing, but returned the dagger to a sheath hidden in his raven-feather cloak. Broadhead warriors would bellow and roar about their victory, but Raven said nothing. As long as he got his payment, he was happy.

It wasn't that simple for me.

Autumn held up the flap and we entered. Teeth were everywhere. Gummy had them in overflowing sacks and clay jugs and bowls on the ground, strung up in lines along the stone walls, or dangling from lines on the ceiling. A fortune in teeth for a toothless man. His two young slaves huddled in the corner, a third cooking some sort of stew over hot coals. What must it be like for them—surrounded by wealth, but not owning their own skins?

Gummy settled on a little stool covered with a blanket. Teeth had been worked into the lining. Probably not comfortable, but he didn't seem to care. All the joy had left him. Now, he had his chin perched in his hand, his eyes half-closed and lost in his wrinkles.

"You know who the Blood-Spiller is." Star stepped carefully around a pile of teeth. "You need to tell us."

"What makes you think that I will?"

"He's taken a child—the son of the Broadhead chieftain. If the little one is hurt, it will plunge Broadheads and the Heap into war. So many will die, you won't be able to count them. There'll be no time for growing plants. And the Blood-Spiller will be behind it all."

"He'll have done what he wanted to do." Gummy sighed. "He'll have stopped me."

"So you know him?" He hadn't mentioned this before—hadn't mentioned anything about it. But he had been lying. Star was smart enough to see it. "Who is he?"

"You shouldn't tell anyone else. Let me know, let you know—and that will be it. If Tale-Spinner, or one of the other storytellers found out..." He shook his head. "It would be the ruin of the planting times to follow, and all the new food. They would discover that there was blood behind it, and the hunting of men." He grabbed Star's arms, his eyes like a beast that had been trapped right before the hunters' spears reached it. "Swear by your Gods. And mine."

Star glared. "You shouldn't ask us anything."

"Talk or there's no more seeds," Autumn added. "That's all."

He swallowed. He reached down, selected a tooth from the pile. A long, yellow specimen. "We all make agreements. Like the fact that this should have value, outside of a mouth. It's a good agreement—it makes sense. Until you step back and look at it. You realize that there is no value here. What is valuable, unquestionably, is our family. And my brother realized that." He let the tooth fall back into its pile with a gentle click. "Bucktooth. That's what we called him, because of his big buckteeth."

"I don't know him." And this was odd. Everyone knew everyone in the Heap. Did Gummy have a little brother? Perhaps he did—but had he gone with the Hill Spirits to dance in the clouds before I arrived?

"You wouldn't. He was—touched by the Gods." Gummy patted his head. "Usually, he should have joined the shamans, but my parents didn't want that. They believed that he could be hidden away, and the gods silenced. They kept him in our cave, brought him food. Occasionally, he went out—so some saw his face. But at night. They raised him in shadow, and that only made the voices of the Gods louder."

Autumn had been listening. "He was listening to all our meetings, wasn't he?"

"The Gods spoke to him and he chose to listen. I know it pained him, but he saw what the planting could do and feared it. I begged him to end his hate—and he begged me." He looked at Star. "Neither of us could be convinced."

Those vision of Broadhead bones. The endless fields—the Thin Ones and all their children, working in the fields and serving fruits and vegetables, spreading them across the face of the earth. And the Tooth King and his children would grow more rich and powerful, while everyone else worked. What kind of future was that?

"Maybe Bucktooth is right." Everyone stared at me as I spoke. "The Gods don't lie. This growing—where will it end? Everyone's children will be slaves to the plants."

"Bucktooth gave out the Wrong Death and stole a child," Star said. "He's not right."

"He's doing what he thinks is right." Gummy sighed. "I won't ask you to spare his life. When you find him—if you find him—let him die quickly. Let it end fast. Give him a—a Right Death. If there is such a thing." He folded his hands. "It's more than I could do."

"But you don't know where he would go?" Star asked.

Gummy shook his head.

I grunted. We knew the name of the Blood-Spiller—but did that make much of a difference? He was still out there, somewhere in the woods, in the land of Eaters and other monsters, with Muddy. If he hadn't filled the boy's mouth with dirt yet. We weren't any closer to finding him.

Star seemed to sense my worry. She patted my shoulder. "We should go see Mother Rat and Mouse. They might know something."

We walked out, Autumn last. She looked back at Gummy. "I'm sorry," he said. "What you're making—I couldn't let you know it was going to be tainted with blood."

Autumn didn't say anything and followed us out.

It took too long to reach the bottom of the Heap and the Rat Cave. Every step, every moment, meant that we were losing Muddy. The Blood-Spiller might already have let his blade do its work, and filled the boy's mouth with dirt. But I couldn't think of that. Couldn't let the fear, cold as the falling snow, clutch my heart and squeeze. We could still do something. We could still save him.

Two guards outside the Rat Cave now. Mother Rat must be worried. They had their rodent-fur vests and ragged scarves. Even as we approached, the bearded guard—the same one I'd met the last time I came here—walked in front of me. "No Fangs. No one comes in at all." He sneered. "And no Broadheads. I heard Tale-Spinner's latest story. You're part of—"

I grabbed him under the arms, lifted him up, and sent him flying into the stone wall beside the cave. He let out a wail before crashing down. His friend, a short Thin Nose with mud-colored hair and a permanently squinting eye, reached to his belt for his own weapon. I grabbed his arm, twisted it, and then slammed my forehead into his face. He squawked and fell flat on his back. Star, Autumn, and I walked inside.

I wasn't in the mood to put flowers in my words.

We entered the first chamber, where Mother Rat usually had her drinks and her music and her games of chance. Now, the tables were empty. The lamps guttered and flickered—they needed more fat to keep burning. Mother Rat stood in the middle, facing Mouse.

And Good Wolf. My dog, as angry as I felt.

Growls left Good Wolf's jaws. Her ears had flicked back and her teeth flashed. A furry lightning bolt, ready to strike. Mother Rat stared back, much calmer than I would be in the same situation. She glanced at us.

"I wondered when you would arrive." Mother Rat brushed her fingers across her face, tracing the line of her scar. "Mouse appeared, and said you would be there. I expected it. You want to find something stolen, so you come to me." She held out her hands. "But I don't know where the Broadhead boy is."

"You know something." Star moved closer to her, striding past Good Wolf. I wasn't sure which was more frightening. "Nothing goes on in this part of the Heap without you knowing. And you will help us."

"Why?" Mother Rat pointed to Good Wolf. "This isn't the first time I've faced the teeth of a beast."

Would roaring at her work? Or maybe throwing something? Smashing the pots and decorations in her cave? No—I could do that, and she wouldn't be scared. Mother Rat was many things, but she didn't scare easily.

"You sold the Blood-Spiller the seeds," Autumn spoke up. "If the Tooth King found out, he'd punish you."

"That's all I did. I sold a seed in exchange for teeth. Nothing more."

"But where did it happen?" Mouse asked, her voice bright—stumbling on a new idea. "Where did he meet you?"

"By the—" Mother Rat stopped—then looked at Star and me. "If I tell you, will you leave?"

"No promises," Star said. "But we'll be doing something else."

Mother Rat nodded back. "Follow." She motioned with her finger and went to the wall. A blanket covered in bark. Thanks to the lowlight, it nearly

"But I don't know where the Broadhead boy is."

matched the texture of the stone. Behind it, a tunnel into darkness. A secret passage. Mother Rat hunched over and led us down. I went next, and I had to hunch over. Rats would have an easier time of scrambling through this tunnel. Good Wolf patted alongside next to me, her fur brushing my leg. Good to have that company. The others followed as the tunnel led down.

It ended in a grotto, where the water met the stone. Water from the Blood River, flowing right into the cave and rushing against the stone. It had brought some ice with it now, which clustered against the stony bank. A few boats rested there—small watercraft bobbing on their ropes, big enough to carry one person at a time, with carved oars resting in them.

A place where anyone could sail in, buy or sell what they needed, and sail away into the woods. A secret mouth of the Heap.

"He came here?" I knelt near the bank, as if I could still smell the Blood-Spiller. "To buy the seeds?"

Mother Rat shrugged. "And floated away."

"Floated…" Star nodded to herself. "That's how he does it. That's how he travels so fast. We were thinking he just ran through the woods, but that's not it at all. He has a boat. Something small and fast, so he can find his victims, carry them away, prepare them, and drop them." She paced on the stone. "So his cave—it will be near the river and it will be in Eater Territory. That helps." She faced me. "We'll find him."

So he wasn't carried by Night Demons after all. Only water. And there was nothing magical about the Blood-Spiller, even if he and Gummy claimed he talked to the Gods. He was just a man, who wore a mask and carried a fine bow and sailed a fine boat.

He could still be found and killed.

That made me feel a little better.

"We're taking these boats." I pointed to the watercrafts. One for me, one for Star, and Good Wolf could ride with us. "There will be no argument."

"There won't be," Mother Rat agreed.

"Mouse—you have to go into the forest. Find the Tooth King. Find White Hair. Tell them what we learned about the river." She bobbed her head, agreeing to it all. "We'll go ahead, in these boats. Try and find the hideout." The place where I had been tied up, and given that strange concoction that let me see the future. That's what we'd find. "And be careful." Ice in my words, brittle and sharp. "I've put you in too much danger already. I will ask the Hill Spirits to guard you—but you be careful too." I looked at Autumn. "She'll go—"

"No." Autumn had already slid into the first boat. "I'm going with you and Star, Red. And Good Wolf. You were looking out for me when Muddy was taken. I need to help find him." And the seeds and the growing—they were her idea. Maybe she blamed herself for the Blood-Spiller too. "Besides, if you get hurt, you'll need help." She hesitated as she crouched in the boat and took the paddle. "And if—if Muddy is hurt, I can heal him."

A skilled healer—you could never turn one down.

But I still didn't like it.

We took the river, heading downstream into the land of the Eaters. Thanks to the Hill Spirits, the current went with us and carried us along. I had to dip my oar in only occasionally, pushing us away from snow gathered on the bank or some rock stabbing out of the water like a beast's horn. Good Wolf sat next to me, pressed close and whining. She didn't mind swimming, but riding in a boat? That was something else. I didn't like it much either. Cold water splashed up and stung my skin and her fur. My mammoth fur cloak helped, but not enough.

But I would endure. There were other things to fear.

Star pointed up ahead. "Eater Territory." There were the skulls, set in the crooks of trees with flowers in the eye-sockets. More colorful flowers, now faded from the cold, dangling in garlands and bands of woven branches over the forest floor. They could be watching us, hidden amongst the boughs and branches. At any moment, their arrows and nets could fly. How far away were the others? How long until we weren't alone?

"What's that?" Autumn asked. "On the bank."

A set of branches, pressed close—standing bold against the snow. But not fallen. They had been arranged.

Star dug her paddle in and floated toward the snowy bank. I joined in, grunting as I stabbed the oar down. Good Wolf leapt out as soon as she could. She splashed her way to the shore. A bit more difficult for me. I jabbed my oar into the water and hauled myself out. Soggy snow crunched under my feet, but I made it up—right to the riverbank.

"Look at this." Star used the Lance of the Skies, still in its covering, to push aside the branches. There it was—a raft, composed of blonde sections of wood held closely together by woven gut-string. A pole rested next to it. The raft had a few clay jugs and some sacks near the middle, where they wouldn't fall off. Star reached for one and peered inside.

Seeds—shining in the fading sunlight.

The same ones that had been in Frog Face's mouth and Gummy's mouth.

I pushed Good Wolf's head closer. She sniffed, her tail wiggling. She had the scent.

"Red—look over here." Autumn pointed to the snow. Footprints—two sets. I hastened over and Star joined me. Bigger prints and smaller prints. The Blood-Spiller and Muddy. Heading further into the woods. Muddy's prints moved away, before being drawn back.

He had tried to escape.

"Gods." Autumn covered her mouth. "Do you think—he can't have already— the boy must be—"

I gripped my spear. "We'll find him." Tracks and scent. They were all Fangs needed. I patted Good Wolf's back and we set off.

CHAPTER SIX
A TIME TO GROW

Silent in the forest. The silence before a storm. It built around us, the first traces of wind slipping down amongst the trees and stirring the snow into whirls and flurries. Somewhere in the sky, the Hill Spirits had grown angry with us—or maybe they were throwing one of their wild feasts, and the energy of it would seep down and make the winds blow loud. Building a blizzard. We had to find Muddy before that, and stop another blizzard of spears and flame from reaching the land.

We struggled through the snowy woods. Autumn stumbled and gasped— unused to long travel, and especially through this weather. Star made her way carefully along. Snow rarely fell in her homeland, but she had mastered it. I handled it well enough, wrapping my mammoth fur cloak tight. Only Good Wolf seemed at home. A wolf in the woods.

She followed the scent and the trail. Winding along through deer trails and past small clearings. Everywhere, the marks of the Eaters. Bones dangling from branches on cords made from the guts of men. Skulls set in knotholes along with garlands of flowers now crumbling in the cold. The remains of heads placed on sticks worked into the soil, frosted and keeping watch. Telling the Eaters that fresh prey had arrived to hunt and devour.

Then, up ahead—a cry. A child's cry.

"Muddy!" I called his name. The trail had widened, going down a slight slope. Somewhere, up ahead, Muddy was alive. And in the clutches of the Blood-Spiller. I forced my legs to run, the fear and guilt rising inside in a sour tide. Feathers of panic dancing against the front of my belly. I'd let him down. Like my father and the other hunters. Like Scribbles and Frog Face.

I ran. Snow flew from my feet. The slope made me go faster.

"Red—wait!" Star shouted for me, but I didn't stop.

Then my foot slammed down and no ground met it. My hide boot cut through a cover of dead leaves. I stumbled and fell, snow spraying. A glimpse of the cold sky. Fingers, hard as stone, around my shoulder. Star, saving my life. Something slicing against my leg.

I wailed louder than the wind. Good Wolf barked back and darted to my side.

Autumn reached us next. "Careful, Red—careful! I have you."

I craned my head. Below me, a pit trap. Sharpened sticks driven into the earth and covered with dead leaves and snow. Star's warning had saved me, but part of my leg had slipped in—and a wooden spike had met it. The point biting into the flesh of my left leg, just above my ankle. Stabbing deep. It hadn't gone through completely, but one look sent pain and dizziness ripping through me. I curled over as a sudden blinding heat met the cold.

"Help me take his leg out. Gently. We'll not tear the wound." Autumn jabbed some herbs from her pouch into her mouth and chewed. "Red—this will hurt."

"You're big—you'll live through it." Star gripped my hand as she reached down. "We lift on three. One—two—" And on two, she lifted.

I wailed. There hadn't been time to give me something to bite on. More intense pain. This time, I did vomit. The ribs from the Cook Cave. They spilled steaming into the snow as I retched and rolled over. Good Wolf ran to them, tail wagging and feasted. But my leg was free. Autumn spat into her hands, reached down, and covered up the wound. She had a tight binding of leather next and went to work.

I let out a little chuckle. "What's so funny?" Autumn asked.

"I wanted your kiss," I said. "I guess I'll have to settle for your spit."

"Fool." She poked my shoulder as she finished tightening. "It should heal. But for a while. You'll limp." She tossed me my spear. "Use this."

I jabbed it into the dirt and pulled myself up. A limp—just like what I had when I came to the Heap. Though that had been my other foot, and went deeper. Was I going to be a crippled in both legs? The Hill Spirits might like that. They liked funny injuries almost as much as they liked funny deaths. At least for now, I could still stand. I settled on the spear, swigged some water to get rid of the taste of vomit and looked further down the trail.

Smoke curled up into the sky ahead. A village. An Eater village.

If they didn't know we were here, then they knew now.

Good Wolf threw back her head and howled. Feet crunched on the snow.

Star spun away from me and faced the woods as the branches shook. Clumps of snow fell down and their shapes emerged. Night Demons slipping out of the shadows. More than I had fingers and toes. These were not like the confident ambushers in the forest—who Star and Raven had killed. They were the best of the Eaters warriors, who defended the cook fires and homes of their village.

They took no chances, but pointed a mass of arrows and spears at us.

Wordlessly, a few moved in. The strongest Eaters, with muscle gained from eating muscles. Star reached for the Lance of the Skies, her fingers coiled on the handle, but did not draw. Good Wolf's howl faded into a growl. I put my hand on her head and shushed her with a rush of air. Her tail drooped as the growl faded.

A towering Eater wearing a vest of dried skin under his wolf-fur robes held out a hand. He had one eye, the other an empty socket. "Big Mouth will want you." He spoke the language of the Heap haltingly, like his mouth was already full. "Give us your weapons and come for us. If the wolf shows its teeth, we'll kill it."

"Don't touch me." Star still had her hand on her weapon and I gripped my spear.

We couldn't kill all of them. Perhaps we could drive a spear through this Eater before the arrows of the others got us. Star looked at me, her teeth gritted, arms taut. All around us, the wind whistled.

An arrow sang. It hummed through the air and settled heavily into the snow.

"Give us your weapons," the big Eater repeated. "Or you die here."

"Star. Red." Autumn walked closer to me. Her hands went to my spear. "Listen to them." I caught her eye. A knowing look there, like I had seen so many times before. She was planning something. Or at least, she was smart enough to know that we'd die if we tried anything. "I don't want to meet the Rider. Not yet."

Star's slackened her grip. She slid the strap of the Lance's scabbard off her back and handed it over. "Don't open it."

The Big Eater grabbed it and looked at me. "You too, Broadhead."

I tossed my spear to him. With nothing to stand on, I'd have to limp—and the cut in my foot ached, the cold making it worse. The pain gnawed at me, but I said nothing. The Big Eater took our clubs next, and a small plant-cutting knife that Autumn carried. He carried it all in a bundle under his arm and pointed down the trail.

He grunted out his order. "Walk."

We set off. Good Wolf stayed close to me and I put my hand on the back of her neck. She growled—but it was a quiet noise. A calmer noise. She was waiting and so was I. Then, we'd both get a chance to sink our teeth into the enemy. But would it be too late for Muddy? I had heard him cry, so he still lived. Or maybe that was just the wind, the Night Demons mocking me and my effort.

I glanced back at Autumn. She slowed her pace, matching the slowness of my limp. The wound gnawing at me still. Her fingers slipped into one of her pouches and drew out a pinch of red herbs. Slowly, she let a few dots trickle down. Brilliant against the snow.

As soon as I saw it, Autumn gripped my arm and pressed her head against my shoulder. Driving my gaze away. She didn't want the Eaters to notice that I had noticed. I looked away, focusing on the trail up ahead. The way the pain gnawed in my foot with each step. The fear in my heart. It wasn't hard.

Would Autumn's plan work? She put her hand in her pouch for another set, and I forced my gaze ahead. She could leave a trail. We had death at the end of ours.

The Eater village nestled at the foot of a big mountain—a snow-covered, sheer monster of dark stone. Only a few trees sprouted along the sides, the black stone showing through gaps in the snow. Not many caves either. If the Eaters had caves, and places where they could hide from the cold to make their lives easier, would they still seek out humans to eat? Or maybe the taste of man's flesh was just too sweet to miss. The Eaters who had come to watch us certainly seemed to think that. They gathered in a crowd outside of their homes, huddling together for the warmth their village didn't offer. They didn't have much. Ragged huts and lean-tos, built around the trees.

And fires.

Four of them, burning in the center of the clearing. Great, roaring bonfires of stacked white wood. Eater children tossed on dead leaves and twigs to keep the blaze going. They had a good smell, the sweet smell of woodsmoke and herbs.

It would probably add flavor to the meat.

Eater hands shoved us to our knees as the big Eater warrior tossed our weapons in a heap in the snow. Two tried to take hold of Good Wolf, a swaybacked Eater wearing a cap made from a cave lion's head grabbing her back while his scrawny friend, who had tattoos of fangs running along his cheeks, tried to put a rope around her muzzle. Good Wolf lunged out and he wailed, pulling back his hand. Two fingers had gone, leaving stumps red and brilliant.

"Too slow! Too slow!" His stoop-shouldered friend laughed and hopped up and down. "She bit you! She bit you!" Like a child's taunt.

The tattooed Eater stumbled away, clutching his bleeding hand and wailing.

Good Wolf growled and tensed. Going for a pounce? I tried to reach and stop her. A stone reached her first, hurled from across the clearing and banging against her nose. Good Wolf dropped and whined, her body shaking. Snow clung to her fur.

"The wolf knows." A creaking, weathered voice from the edge of the crowd. "The wolf knows the joy that is found within meat."

I held Good Wolf, who whimpered now. A broad-shouldered figure had stepped out of the crowd. There was something wrong with his face. It didn't fit right, and he had lips inside his lips. Then I realized what it was. He wore a mask of another human face, sliced off and tanned and held to his face with cords. It had been treated and tattooed with bright red and blue lines, making the lips and eyes bigger and bolder. The frozen features didn't change, making him look calm. He had no hair to speak of, and wore a ragged vest and coat of aurochs fur, speckled with ornaments of bone.

A Night Demon, if I'd ever seen one.

"Big Mouth," Star murmured.

"That is my name." Big Mouth walked over to us. "A warrior from the south. And a Broadhead. Look at you. Look at the strength there." He shuddered suddenly and twisted to the side, spinning next to the fire—perilously close to the blaze. "If you only knew the joy of meat, you'd embrace it. You'd never want to eat anything else."

"I don't know," Autumn said. "Steamed apples taste good."

"You have no place here." He sprang closer to us and knelt down, facing Autumn. His finger lashed out, grabbing at her ear. He tugged and she screamed—then he pushed her back, his palm going over her face. I stood—to tackle him, to hit him. Anything to make it stop. Star grabbed my arm. "I've heard of you. You and your friends. The Tooth King, the one with no teeth. You want to eat plants. How will you ever gain any strength?" He pulled his hand back. "How will you get the Gods to love you?"

"What are you talking about?" Star demanded.

"They love me. They put fire into my head." He touched his fingers to his forehead. Or to the forehead of the face he wore. "And within that fire, I see everything. I can see your power, coming off of you like smoke. That's what I'm going to take when I eat you."

"I will you show you my power right now." I folded my hands into fists. "Just give me a chance, Big Mouth."

"I'll cut you open, Broadhead." He pointed to my belly. "And I'll put rocks heated in the fire inside of you, to cook you just the right way. I'll drizzle on the herbs to make you taste right, and I'll take the first bites while you're still alive. I'll let the women suck out your eyeballs. The children will make toys out of your fingers. The wolf we'll tie to a tree and let starve. Maybe, we'll give her some pieces of you—and she'll eat them happily. She knows what you'll find out in the end."

A rustling in the crowd. Big Mouth stood and pointed. "And I promise, you won't be eaten alone."

The Eaters parted. A dark form slipped through, coming from one of the houses. He had his hand on Muddy's wrist. The boy had a blackened eye, the bruise just beginning to darken—hidden in shadow by his tangle of dark hair. The figure wore a cloak made from the skin of a black cave lion. He looked at us through a mask made from the skull of a giant ape.

The Blood-Spiller. We'd found him at last.

"Muddy." I spoke in the Broadhead speech. "Don't be afraid. Don't worry. We will find a way out of here."

"Red." He nodded to me—not whimpering or crying. Just staring and trying his best to be brave. Seeing me, and Autumn, and Star, had to be the first bit of hope he had. Even if we were unarmed and lying before the fire, about to go under the knives and teeth of the Eaters. "You'll rescue me?"

"That's what I'm here to do."

The smile came suddenly—a child's smile.

"What are you saying to him?" The Blood-Spiller tugged Muddy's arm back, and he winced.

Now I stood, and my voice came out a screech. "If you hurt him—"

"What?" The Blood-Spiller asked. "What will you do?" He put his hand on Muddy's shoulder. "I gave you a chance and you didn't take it. You chose the way of growing. It is only fair that your meat should be on the fire."

I stared back. The Blood-Spiller was right. Nothing I could say, no threats I could make, would change that we were in their power. A whole village of Eaters stood between us and freedom.

I sat down, next to Autumn. Muddy still looked at me—still expecting me to save him. Like my father had expected me be there, when we hunted that bear in its cave.

Big Mouth had settled on his haunches, before the fire. "I want the boy to be eaten first. He looks boney. And Broadheads always have too much muscle— makes the meat stringy. I'll slice him thin, smoke him—dry him out over warm ashes. We'll chew on him between bites of her." He pointed to Autumn. "Bring him here and I'll snap his neck and start carving."

"We can't eat him. The Gods wouldn't like that. I need to fill his mouth with his dirt and leave him by the river for everyone to find." Now, he whined. "I need to send my message. That's what we agreed, Big Mouth, when I came to you."

"And there's something you need to know." Big Mouth tossed some more kindling onto the fire. The blaze rose, sending up a crackle of sparks and smoke. "If you are in my village, you must learn to share your kills."

Star leaned closer to me. "This is good."

"What?"

"They're putting fire into their words—arguing. Could be our chance." She pointed to the weapons. "Think you can reach them, with your foot?"

It still ached. I didn't know.

Then, Good Wolf howled again. Her tail spun. The Eaters didn't like that. Several covered their ears as the high, trilling sound echoed over the trees and matched the cold blow of the wind.

"Keep your wolf silent!" Big Mouth pointed to her with a long-bladed flint carving knife. "Quiet her!"

I patted her, and followed the point of her nose. Shapes in the forest. Snow crunching under their feet. And then shrill cries, matching Good Wolf's howl.

The Broadheads had arrived. They hurried through the forest, all the Frost warriors, along with the Hillmen. Song led them—the bravest in the hills and the best huntsman. He had his spear in his arm, point at the ready, his shrill cry coming in a musical song. Rock followed him, and then White Hair and her finest fighters.

"Mother of mine!" Muddy called to his mother.

She burst out of the woods, frost falling around her, the great, two-handed club held high and ready to be brought down on skulls, shoulders, and bellies. The red juice of crushed berries had been placed in thin lines along her cheeks, forehead, and down the bridge of her nose, like she was already covered in the blood of her enemies.

"Muddy—my heart beats for you." She stood at the edge, her warriors around her. "We will be home soon. I swear on the Frost Spirits."

The Eaters wailed and reached for their own weapons. They had chopping axes, long knives, and short stabbing spears. Bows and spear-throwers, with human bone serving a role in the construction of many weapons. All the cunning of Thin Noses, paired with a monstrous appetite.

"Come near and he dies." Big Mouth scrambled up. He reached the Blood-Spiller and aimed his knife back—pointing the tip at Muddy's tear-streaked face. "One step and I take his throat."

A smart decision. He didn't want a battle near in his village.

White Hair spun the club to face him. "I'll break before you die. Let him go."

"Walk away and send a messenger." Big Mouth moved the knife closer to Muddy, jabbing the tip into his cheek. "We might let him go. But take your warriors away or I'll kill him now."

For a Thin Nose, it might have worked. But not a Broadhead. Our hearts are too big. We loved too fiercely. And when those we loved are threatened, we do not think. We act.

White Hair roared and charged to save her son.

Big Mouth hurled the knife, throwing it expertly. It spun, end over end, and stabbed straight into White Hair's shoulder. But by then, she wasn't the only one charging.

The other Broadheads raced in, crying as one. Song led their charge, swinging a club of wood and stone above his head. The big Eater, the warrior who had captured us, reared up to meet him and caught the club in the side of the skull. Bone shattered and he went down, right into the fire. Sparks and burning chunks of wood flew as the other Broadheads raced in.

Arrows and spears met them, soaring from the Eater ranks before the battle got in close.

I rolled over, Good Wolf barking next to me. Star was already up and moving toward our weapons. Someone screamed—a child's voice. Eater or Muddy? I couldn't tell. Couldn't understand anything in the sudden chaos.

The tattooed Eater, with fangs on his cheeks, burst from the smoke. Running toward Star as she grabbed for her weapons. Good Wolf had taken his fingers, but that didn't slow him down as he aimed his spear. I ran to Star, my bad foot aching. I would be too slow.

A trio of arrows plunged into the Eater's chest. He dropped, his blood racing down and falling over the snow. Not Eater arrows.

The arrows of Heap men.

"Wipe them from the earth!" Bug Eyes' cry. I looked to the edge of the clearing. "Slay the Eaters of man! Glory to the Tooth King!"

"Glory to the Tooth King!" More voices took up the call. Purple Plume hurried in, leading the Feathers in all their fine clothes. They looked beautiful and they fought well.

All around us, the Eaters that couldn't fight ran for shelter in the huts and tents or scrambled into the shelter of the woods. Broadheads fought up close, stabbing with spears or swinging their clubs and fists. Arrows whistled from everywhere as Purple Plume's archers matched the bows of the Eaters. Those four fires crumbled as bodies fell against them and burning chunks of wood and sparks hit the ice and steamed.

There was plenty of blood to be spilled.

I had never been in a battle before. When the Frost Tribe raided our homes, I had been too young and when the Heap warred with Bull Island, I had been weak. Now, I felt like I was drowning in a storm-wracked sea of fire, blood, and death. I stayed next to Autumn, who crouched low as Good Wolf barked. An Eater stumbled past us, an arrow in his chest, and bleeding as he struggled along. A Broadhead dropped down, hands at his throat—his blood boiling through his fingers and soaking his beard and the snow beneath.

Nothing but the Wrong Death.

Star at least, who had been a warrior in her home in the south, still had her senses. "Red!" She hurried to the mass of our weapons, and armed up, then tossed me my spear and my club. I caught them both. "Come on. We find the boy. We find White Hair. Get them out of here."

"Red—" Autumn stood. "Your foot—"

"Stay here!" I pointed to the trees. "Hide. Fight, if an Eater gets close. But stay hidden!" I clicked my tongue. Good Wolf leapt to my side with a growl.

Then Star and I dove deeper into that storm.

We hurried through the battle to the side of the central fire. Hard to see anything in the smoke and chaos. I stepped over a fallen Broadhead, my bad foot jabbing against his belly and stinging painfully—and then White Hair herself stumbled out of the smoke. She'd lost her poleaxe and the knife remained in her shoulder, plunged in deep. The carved handle remained, jabbing out, and leaving a trail of blood from the ragged wound. She glanced at me and her eyes burned bright with hate. Deserved hate. I'd lost her son.

Then Big Mouth tackled her.

They crashed to the ground together, near the remains of the fire. He was on top, his hand going for the knife in her shoulder—jabbing it down. Even in the chaos of the battle, her scream sounded loud. She got her hands around his throat and squeezed, even as he twisted the blade free. It left her in a shower of blood just as Star and I reached them.

Big Mouth slipped off of her, hoisting up his knife. He danced back, holding it with the back hand and making a few swings. Wild gestures—the madness in him. "I can see it!" He sliced the air. "The light inside of me. The burning.

The gift of flesh!" Inside his mask, his lips and teeth had formed a crazy grin. "I'm going to eat you all."

Star pulled the Lance of the Skies from its sheath and went for a stab—he darted back—until Star spun it around and stabbed it through his foot. It cut through and pinned him to the snowy ground.

"Red!" She worked the point down, making screams leave Big Mouth's mouth. "Get to White Hair! Help her!"

I knelt beside her. Got her hand onto the wound. A long and bloody gash. Her grip already weak. I forced her hand down, pushing bundled and torn white bear fur in to staunch the bleeding. Still, the crimson crept through my fingers and made my hands slick. The fur wouldn't hold.

I was no healer. I didn't know what to do.

"Hold on, Red! Hold on!" Autumn. She came through the chaos. Running through the flames—leaping over a stunned Eater and Feather as they thrashed together on the ground. Good Wolf barked and dashed to her. She slid to a halt and replaced my pressure. More of her healing tools coming to hand. "It's long, but not deep." She worked carefully, already shoving more plants in her mouth to chew. "Hold her still, Red. Just a bit more."

White Hair moaned. "Muddy." She breathed out his name.

Star shouted. I looked up from White Hair. Big Mouth had brought his knife up and slashed against her shoulder. It cut mammoth fur and reached skin. The knife came away bloody. He grabbed for her throat, trying to hold her in place as he went for another downwards slash—using the long knife like an axe—aiming to plant the blade in her forehead.

His knife came down. I wasn't there for her.

But Star lunged up and caught his wrist. She gripped it tight. Her muscles strained under her coat as she shoved it up. Big Mouth saw what was happened. He opened his mouth to yell and tried to get away.

But the Lance of the Skies pinned his foot. He wailed and stumbled.

She rammed the point of the blade into the bottom of Big Mouth's chin. Where his head met his throat. The blade pierced through mask and skin and jabbed up. Big Mouth's mouth opened. A glimpse of his tongue, severed through. The blade kept going and the tip cut through the roof of his mouth. He slumped down and fell to the snow. Choking and rolling as blood squirted out.

Star drew the Lance of the Skies from his foot and drove it down with both hands into Big Mouth's head. Through the eye socket of the mask and the eye socket of his face. He stopped his writhing.

"Let go, Red." Autumn's voice—it sounded far away, but she was right next to me. "I've got her. Let go."

I pulled my hands away. Star stumbled over and joined us. Autumn looked

She rammed the point of the blade. . .

up, her red hair a tangle. "Big Mouth—I'm glad you killed him."

"He'd tried to eat too much." She shrugged. "And choked."

Thin Nose humor. I didn't understand.

Good Wolf perked up with a growl as Purple Plume, locked in battle with the swaybacked Eater, stumbled by. They fought for Purple Plume's decorated spear, like two children trying to pull a favorite toy out of their hands. I pointed to the Eater and whistled and Good Wolf leapt at him. A powerful leap. Her jaws flashed and took him in the arm, tugging it back and making him lose his grip as he wailed. Purple Plume ripped his spear free, spun it around, and drove it through the Eater's chest.

He wasn't the leader of the Tooth King's guards just for wearing pretty feathers.

The Eater dropped and Purple Plume ripped his spear free. He looked at me at nodded. "The Broadheads—they fight well. We'll win." He stared at White Hair. "We must take her to the clearing's edge. To the trees, with the Tooth King. She'll be safe there."

Autumn took one arm and I grabbed the other, while Star handled the legs. "Just a little more, White Hair," Autumn said. "I don't know if you even understand, but hold on—just a little more."

White Hair mumbled a single word in response. "Muddy…"

We got her through the chaos of the village. Purple Plume cleared a way with jabs of his spear. Rock and Song emerged from the smoke, their weapons bloody. Both had taken wounds, but they could still stand and fight. Their clubs, Purple Plume's spear, and Good Wolf's jaws were all the help we needed. I stepped on dead bodies.

Then we reached the trees. Away from the smoke and the killing. There, the Tooth King sat on his litter, his slaves huddled around him—guarded by three Feathers with heavy shields of carved and painted wood, decorated with specks of shiny stone and teeth. Those shields parted and the Feathers let us through. Autumn drew closer to a tree and we set White Hair down. Letting her sit upright, leaning against the frosted wood.

"Give her a blanket." The Tooth King himself had been swaddled in sealskin, fox fur, and pelts from numerous other animals. Enough to make several tents. A Feather with a feather in his broad-brimmed hat hastened to obey, and put a leopard skin around White Hair. "What about the boy?" The Tooth King's gaze went to me.

Because I had been asked to protect him, and failed.

I couldn't answer.

"We lost him." Star sighed. "Same with the Blood-Spiller. They must have run when the fighting started. But we can track them." Then she winced. She dropped lower.

The arrow wound the Blood-Spiller had given her. The knife of Big Mouth. Her injuries were taking a toll.

Autumn ran to her. "She needs to stay here. She needs to rest." Her eyes met mine. "Same with you, Red. You and that foot. You'll have to send someone else."

But I could walk—even if it was a limp. And I had something that could help. I dug into the satchel, hidden under my robes. A chunk from the boar ribs that I'd bought for Muddy, back on the Trader's Ledge. It seemed to have happened many seasons ago. I pulled out the rib, knelt down, and held it up to Good Wolf. The boy's scent must remain. She sniffed, chewed on it, and panted. Her head bobbed up and down as her ears tented.

Oh yes. She had the scent.

"Red, you can't." Autumn looked up from Star. "You've been injured, you're tired. The Blood-Spiller's fresh, and this is home—and he has a prisoner. We'll find him later. We can still save—"

I reached out. Brushed her hair over her head. "He's spilled enough blood. And he'll hurt Muddy if we wait. Send more than one and he'll slip away—or kill the boy. It should be me. It must be me." Even in the cold, she sweated.

White Hair groaned. I knelt closer to her, the pain still gnawing in my foot.

Her breath came weak. "The Frost Spirits will guide you. They know what is just." Her fingers fixed on my wrist. Still incredibly strong. "Save my son."

"I will." A promise—but this time, would I keep it?

Good Wolf howled and pushed at my hand. Eager to hunt. So was I.

We started off toward the mountain.

We followed the trail toward the mountain, leaving the battle behind. It still raged behind me, the heat and crackle of flame and the shouts, shrieks, and cries of war flashing over my shoulder. The sky was still gray, with only a little shadow creeping in. Barely any time had passed since the Eaters had caught us and White Hair had started the battle. Lifetimes went by in moments once the spears started to fly. But that was good.

It meant that the Blood-Spiller and Muddy couldn't have gone far.

Good Wolf led me to a slope, which reached a narrow ledge. She pawed along, then stopped and sat down. Her nose pointed the way. Up ahead, a cave loomed—dark and terrible. A wound, carved in the dark stone of the mountain. The Blood-Spiller must have gone into the darkness. I had some animal skins draped in fat and wrapped that around my club. After that, flint sent down sparks and got the torch burning. All Fangs had to carry the makings of torches.

You never knew when we'd have to go into the dark.

I hoisted it high and walked ahead, Good Wolf at my side. We entered the shadow. The torchlight mingled with shafts of cold sun creeping in through gaps in the cave roof and walls. Not the best, but I could see enough. Bones lying thick on the ground. Gnawed, broken, and picked clean. The Blood-Spiller's work? Impossible. There was an arm that could only come from a rhino. The Blood-Spiller couldn't have killed that.

A whine from Good Wolf. I stopped and hoisted the torch. Letting the light shine a little further into the cave.

There, near the back. A great lump of living darkness. Moving slightly. The outline of a hump, of brown fur stained with the dirt of the cave. Eyes closed, a head as big as the moon resting between two paws.

A cave bear.

The old fear came back. The cave bear wasn't only an animal. That wasn't what had made me run, and leave my father and the other hunters. It was everything cruel about the world. The cold that never vanished or the heat that put an ache in your skull. The flame in an empty stomach, that would never end until you found enough food.

Everything that made life hard, given claws and teeth and sent into the world to kill.

My legs went still. I couldn't go any further. What would be the point? The trail had led to a cave with a cave bear in it. The Blood-Spiller and Muddy were not here. Only death, waiting for in those jaws and claws. A single bite, a single swing, and there wouldn't be enough left for even the Hill Spirits to gather away. My injured leg only made me easier prey. I clutched the torch and leaned against the wall, forcing breath into my lungs.

Good Wolf pushed her muzzle against my hand. Her nose went to the wall. There, further along—a hole in the wall. Another cave.

So the Blood-Spiller had made his home near a bear's cave. It made sense. Just like putting himself near the Eaters. The bear would warn him of anyone who came close. He probably used other entrances, other tunnels, to make his way to his hideout. Probably, one of those was where he had brought me the night he killed Scribbles.

A low groan from the bear. A strangely gentle noise. A quiet stirring.

The bear was asleep. They would do that—stuff themselves, find a cave, and slumber through the winter until the warm days of spring woke them up. This cave bear had probably just finished stuffing himself and was settling down.

Not a monster. Not all the cruelty of the world. Just a beast that needed to nap.

I breathed in deep. Forced away the pain in my leg. One hand held the torch and the other pushed down on Good Wolf's muzzle, making sure she didn't bark. The bear slept—but was it a light sleeper? We would have to be quiet.

We crept by. I put my back to the wall. The torch felt slick in my hands. Sweat on my palms and down by neck. Terribly cold in that cave. I kept going. Step by step. The bear groaned, the rise and fall of its chest half-hidden in the darkness. But it didn't wake. We reached the gap in the wall and slipped through the second cave.

A slope, rising. Jagged stone below. I let go of Good Wolf and she loped ahead. Now, my leg truly ached. Every step made me wince. I kept going. Further up, and then to the top—where more firelight burned.

The ape skull waited for me at the top.

"Red!" Muddy's voice, shouting a warning just as Good Wolf growled.

Then a slim tube appeared below the skull, and air rushed. A gentle pinch in my shoulder. My hand shot up and grabbed at the needle. I pulled it free. The same jagged thorn he had stabbed me with earlier. Letting his Night Demon claws rip into my skull and spill his spittle into my mind. I closed my eyes.

When I opened them again, the walls were made of bone. Broadhead bone. Broadhead skulls set amongst them. Gathering dust—abandoned for many, many seasons. This was the end that awaited my people.

No—shake off the fear. There was one Broadhead, an innocent, who needed you. Who you had promised to protect, and failed. Like you had failed so many. Do what a Fang had to do.

I doubled my pace. Charging up the steps. Broadhead skulls crunched under my feet. I didn't care. Swings of the torch made the shadows dance as I forced myself up. Good Wolf ran with me. The ape skull moved back, vanishing into the shadow. I surged after it, giving the torch a swing that made the air hum.

The Blood-Spiller dodged it. He hurried back, further into his workshop. Now, he was one shadow, split only with white. The darkness pulsed off of him—a true Night Demon. Muddy crouched behind him, pressed against the wall. Just another prize, a captured animal waiting to be carved up, along with the dried carcasses and roots dangling from the ceiling.

The Blood-Spiller grabbed his fine bow. He had an arrow to the string—no, a writhing serpent. Venom spilled from bright fangs at the end of the arrow as the Blood-Spiller had it at full draw. He'd put that arrow through my throat and end me.

"No—you will not hurt him!" Muddy, speaking with the fierceness of his mother.

He hurled a stinking berry, one I had bought him in the Trader's Ledge, right at the Blood-Spiller's face. It hit the skull mask and split on the bone. The stench came. Even I could smell it, pinching and rotting in my nostrils.

The bowstring sang. The arrow hummed past me. The wind of it tickled my shoulder and it cracked into the wall.

"Broadhead wretch!" The Blood-Spiller's hand went to his mask. He tugged it down. The skull came away, grinning as it clattered on the stone floor. Shadow still clung to him. He looked up. For a moment, the vision faded.

A normal face. The skin pale, the eyes green. A frightened look to his lips, pressed together in the fear that everything was falling apart. And yes—a pair of buckteeth. No Night Demon at all. Just a Thin Nose who didn't mind giving others the Wrong Death.

He grabbed Muddy's arm and twisted. The boy wailed and the Blood-Spiller smacked him with the handle of his fine axe. He hoisted it up. "Come closer and I'll bring it down. I will split his skull. I promise it." He glared at me, the whine creeping into his voice. "We should have been friends, Red. You've seen what I've seen. You're smart. For a Broadhead. You know the doom that waits in those seeds. Help me kill the little one. We'll pour in the dirt. We'll start a war and save everyone."

He had the boy—he had the advantage. I couldn't reach him before the axe struck Muddy. Good Wolf, growling at my side—was she that fast? Could I risk it? Even a wolf couldn't outrun a Night Demon.

But he wasn't a Night Demon. He was a man.

A man with a name.

"You're a sad and weak Thin Nose," I said. "Hidden in the back of your cave. I pity you. I wish your brother had been kinder. I wish there was something better for you. If I knew you, even with the voice of the Gods in your ears, I still could have called you friend. I would have been happy to know you, Bucktooth."

"How—how did you—" He stopped, and the axe lowered.

I clicked my tongue. Good Wolf leapt at him. She flew through the air, teeth flashing, and there was lightning crackling in her fur and stars shining in her eye. She became a comet, which smashed into Bucktooth and knocked him down.

"Muddy!" I called to the boy and he scrambled to me. I took his hand. Safe—alive. I needed to keep him that way.

Bucktooth blocked Good Wolf's jaws with his arm. She sunk her teeth in deep, and the blood coursed down in rivers. Then he swung his axe and kicked out. The blow settled against Good Wolf. She whimpered and pulled away.

No—not her.

But Good Wolf turned around and ran to me. Blood slick on the side of her pelt. But still alive.

"Come on, Muddy." I patted his shoulder. "Just a little more. White Hair's waiting for you."

"Oh." We started down the slope, slipping over the jagged stones. Light pulsed in the walls, which moved and shifted. Muddy and I going down a giant throat, into some waiting stomach. "Good." A whine crept into his voice. "I tried to fight him, Red. Mouse—I couldn't help her."

"She's well. And you did just what you were supposed to. You're so brave, Muddy. Like a warrior should be."

"Like a warrior should be," he repeated.

I steered him down the slope. He shivered—from fear or the cold, I couldn't say. Good Wolf loped along as we made our way down the steps. Bucktooth still lived. Fair enough. But the boy was more important. I had to get him out, get him to safety in the woods—and then go back and give what the Blood-Spiller had given to Frog Face and Scribbles.

He had a Wrong Death coming to him.

The cave mouth ahead of us. A few more steps and we'd be there. I gave Muddy a push, sending him ahead. "Stay near the cave wall." I dropped my voice. "Stay quiet." Let the bear sleep. Let us get away. I gave him a little push. "Just a little further and—"

Something heavy took me in the shoulder. I went down, dropping onto my belly. Muddy screamed. Why wasn't he running? Good Wolf growled and then whimpered. Another blow settling into her—going wet. I rolled over. There was Bucktooth. No mask—but darkness in his face. He had his knife up. The blade gleamed as it came down. I tried to twist to the side, but he took me in the upper chest.

The blow—the sharpness of it—pushed all the breath away.

"Lay there, Red." Bucktooth stood up, his arm bleeding, as I crumpled. "Lay there and die. I'll be back to put the dirt in your mouth." He stood and stumbled towards Muddy—who still hadn't run. "And you—I've been waiting all day to put an end to you."

Something roared in the darkness. All that noise, all that blood spilled. No bear could sleep on.

My father looked down at me. All the scars on his face, shifting as he scowled. "Coward." He spat out the word, just as he had before. It settled on me like a blow.

"Red." Another voice. Autumn's. Soft in my ears. "He was wrong. There's no one braver. Your heart is big—and big hearts make you brave."

I rolled over. Forced myself to stand. The spear rested at the entrance. I grabbed it and ran to Bucktooth. He had the axe up, Muddy in front of him—and turned to stare at me.

I rammed the spear into his gut and pushed it as hard as I could.

He gasped and sunk down. I grabbed his shoulder—I spun him around and shoved.

He fell before the cave bear.

The claws came down. A bite that took away half of his face and ended his scream. Deep growls from the bear. Happy for a little more food before winter's sleep.

Let the beast eat.

It didn't pursue. Already full. Or too tired. Or because there was no monster there at all.

I went to Muddy and took his hand. Good Wolf hopped next to us. We limped out—three hurt, broken, weak figures. Back out into the snow, and away from that mountain.

Down to the Eater village, now burned and gone. Broadheads raised their shrill voices and cheered as the Feathers shook their spears to the sky. I led Muddy back to the trees, where the Tooth King stood next to White Hair, in her blanket, leaning against the tree.

"Mother White Hair." Muddy ran to her.

But her arms didn't rise for an embrace.

He sank down by her knees and cried—the pure, terrible weeping of a child.

I limped over and looked at the Tooth King, his face grave. "The wound was too deep, Red. She didn't make it."

I tumbled down as well. Autumn and Star ran to me. Autumn wept. "It doesn't make sense—the wound—it wasn't that deep." She blamed herself, and then her eyes went to my wound. "You're hurt, Red." Autumn's hands, moved quick as my legs gave way. "Hold still. We'll help you. You'll make it." But she sounded far away. Instead, my eyes went to Muddy. I had saved him. But White Hair was gone. The boy would be alone now, even as he took White Hair's place.

"Muddy," I whispered his words. "The Frost Clan is yours."

He didn't hear me. He cried for his lost mother instead.

A season passed. Winter came cruel, but it faded, as it always did. Spring arrived. The snow melted from the trails and bridges of the Heap, and we left our homes and sang around the fires to celebrate the return of the sun. The Elephant Mother, emerging from her long journey to look after her children— that's what the Thin Ones said. I knew it was the Hill Spirits, dancing closer to our world and bringing light and laughter with them. But whatever the case, we had snowmelt in the river and enough game from the hunts to fill our bellies.

But some things never changed. Star and I walked through the Trader's Ledge, making our usual walk around the Heap to see if trouble occurred— and it did. "Stop!" A shout from Cook. "He didn't pay for that!"

Squints, who had once fought over a dead monkey, had grabbed a hunk of meat, steaming from the fire, and dashed off. Panting as he weaved through the stalls. He leapt over a line of clay pots, scrambled around a fishmonger's stall, and neared us.

Star crossed to him and jabbed out her leg. He went sprawling, clutching the boar close.

I ambled over to him and rolled him over. "Squints." My new spear jabbed at him. "You're stealing now?"

"I'm—I'm hungry." He clutched the meat close.

The hollowness in his eyes, the desperation in his eyes. Yes—that was hunger. I'd felt it and it put fire in my heart. "Here." I dug out a few teeth and offered them to Squints. "Next time, ask. We shouldn't go hungry. Give this to Cook and ask for more."

He held the teeth close and stood. A slight nod. "Thank you, Red." A quiet mumble.

"Steal again and you'll lose your hand." Star waved to him as he hastened away. She patted my shoulder. "You're too nice, Red. You grow soft."

"Maybe I could use a little softness."

Muddy certainly could. I had tried to be there for him, as he stood in the Tooth King's cave about halfway through winter. He looked absurd in the white robes of a chieftain, blue paint shining on his expectant face—trying to look as grave and serious as he could while I translated the Tooth King's request.

He had agreed to them. The Heap got the Flowering Fields. They'd deliver fruit to the Frost Clan and the Stone Clan, in exchange for the land. I had told Muddy it was right. It would keep hunger from the Frost Clan.

But it would lose them their hunting grounds. It would keep them in the cold mountains, and away from the growing lands of the Heap.

If the other Men of Frost disagreed, they didn't say it. They were loyal to White Hair—and they would be loyal to her son.

Oh yes. By the Hill Spirits, I wanted to be kinder.

We neared a fire built on the center of the Trader's Ledge, where a crowd had gathered to stand against a spring chill. Spinner worked at her trade, telling a story. Star and I listened for a moment, and it only took that long to realize the story.

Spinner's friend hoisted up the puppet of the stuffed badger—my puppet. "The Broadhead Hero, strongest of his people—half-wild, but tamed by the Heap—and fighting for justice!" She waved smoke over the badger, and another puppet joined the battle, bearing the monkey skull. "He tracked the Blood-Spiller, with the young Broadhead boy in his arms." A little doll with some squirrel fluff served for Muddy. "And when he was lost, he called to the beasts for help."

Another of Spinner's friends played the part of the bear. No puppet for him. Just a full costume. Sloth fur and a bear skull. He appeared out of the smoke, doing his best roar. Children in the audience gasped and huddled close to their parents as fake claws ripped the Blood-Spiller away. Berry juice squirted out, onto the flames.

"And so, the Heap was saved—by its strangest champion." Spinner spread her hands and went into a deep bow. The audience hooted and cheered. The bear removed his head—only a hat—and held it out to collect teeth. Spinner urged the payment before glancing in our direction. She waved to the audience and joined us.

"Did you like the show?" Her hands linked with Star's.

"Terrible." Star hugged her close. Their kiss came fierce. They'd been together since winter. "You didn't have the bloody battle. The deaths we suffered. The injuries Red and I got. There seemed to be even less truth than usual."

"Maybe the truth doesn't earn as many teeth." Spinner shrugged and waved to me. "Hello, Red. I've told this story often enough. I need another. Where's the next Blood-Spiller? The next monster? My stories need a little more spice."

"My life is fine," I replied. "Without more spice."

"Well, you just wait, Red." Spinner gave me a wink. "The stories will come to you."

An excited hum, followed by a chorus of yips, cut off my reply. Good Wolf ran to me. A little slower now—a hitch in her step thanks to the wounds the Blood-Spiller had given her. But now, her pups were big enough to go with her. A whole pack of them, dashing over to me and Star and leaping up, their tongues dancing. I knelt down and petted and received the lick of the pups until my cheek and beard were slick and my hands hurt.

Mouse approached behind them. She'd been giving them their daily walk around the Heap. When dogs got big, they needed their walks—and Good

Wolf's pups were getting bigger and bigger.

"Red—you should go to the Heap's Bottom." Her face shone with excitement. "The growers are back!"

The growers. Autumn and those that followed her, who would had gone to the Flowering Fields. Finally, they'd returned. I stood up, my hand settled between Good Wolf's ears to scratch. "And Autumn?"

"She's with them, as far as I can see." Mouse pointed down the trail, leading to the Heap's Bottom. "The Tooth King himself will be there to greet them. Many people of the Heap will come and greet the Growers. Like they are warriors returning from a battle or hunters from the field." And in a way, they were. They'd be battling starvation, and creating a new source of food that would better everyone.

"Put sunlight into your heart, Red." Star motioned to the Trader's Ledge. "There's no trouble here. We should go and greet them."

"I would like that," I agreed. I clicked my tongue and the dogs followed in a group. "You can come too, Mouse. There are times when you get a chance to witness great things—the hands of the Hill Spirits in daily life. Like when they sunder a great mountain, cause an avalanche, or flood a valley. This will be like that—but it's human hands that are changing fate." But I wanted to see the returning Growers for another reason.

Autumn would be with them.

I tapped my spear against the stone and started for the causeway leading down. The dogs followed me. Spinner gave Star a final kiss and returned to her trade, while Mouse darted along at our side. We took the slope down, made the turns over the switchbacks, and reached the final slope. Soon, we were at the bottom of the Heap.

Near the bridge overlooking the Blood River, and the huts of the fisherwomen. Some of their catches lay dead and drying, their nets, rods, and spears set up in the warming sun. Not far from here, not so long ago, Frog Face's body had been in the riverbank by the mud, and Star and I had pulled him out. Now, what had caused Frog Face's Wrong Death had come to pass.

The most powerful and richest of the Heap had come out to greet the Growers. Gummy stood there, leaning on a carved staff. Raven next to him, still guarding the old man. The Feathers formed two lines on the side of the trail, hoisting up their plumed spears. And there was the Tooth King, sitting on his litter—his keen eyes staring into the distance. He had one of his pet cats perched on his lap, and there was something about the half-closed, contented look in his eye that matched that of the beast.

A few musicians waited, their drums, flutes, and gut-string harps ready to play.

The Growers emerged from the woods and crossed over the bridge. Ten of them and ten again. They had the marks of spring sun on their faces and arms, and dirt on their hands. Some stumbled or staggered—pausing to sip from their waterskins. Fatigue—it clung to them. And after weeks of planting and tending, how could they not be tired? Even more Growers stayed in the field, and this group would be going back soon enough to keep tending the plants. They'd need to pour in the water, to keep animals away, to tend and grow the fruit trees and roots.

Slaves to the soil. Like Bucktooth had said.

Music greeted them, and flowers thrown down from the upper levels of the Heap. Pink petals drifting down in a pale, floating shower.

"Our future is here!" The Tooth King raised his voice. All fell silent. "Our future, to be found in seeds and soils. We plant, we grow, we harvest—and then, we will eat well, every night. It will be hard at first. It will always be hard. But with so much food, we can grow and grow like the plants in the earth—until we spread across all the world and make the Gods amazed with our glory."

"Glory to the Tooth King! Glory to the Tooth King!" Everyone cheered.

"Glory to the Growers!" The Tooth King called, and this cry was repeated.

The Growers crossed the bridge, smiling and greeting their friends as the music rose. I searched the crowd. Yes—there she was. That tangle of red hair, like fire—the freckles moving on her face as she smiled. She embraced a fellow Grower, a Thin Nose with a big straw hat, before bowing to the musicians and hurrying over to the crowd.

Then she spotted me.

She dashed over. Good Wolf and the dogs bounded up to meet her, and Autumn laughed as they danced around her. She petted them and watched their tails wag and looked at me, a smile on her face that came from the joy of playing with dogs.

Oh, there was enough fire in my heart at the sight of her to burn down the world.

She walked over and we hugged each other. A kiss on my lips, my cheeks, my forehead. I ran my hand through her hair.

"I missed you, Red. How are your injuries?"

"Healing well. And how was the growing?" I looked at her hands. Dirt stuck deep in her fingernails.

"Not much growing now. The plants need time. We plant now, tend them during the long summer months when they can get the sun they need, and then pluck the fruits and dig up the roots during fall." She hesitated. "Collect. Take. *Harvest.*" A new word, and unsteady on her tongue. "Oats and roots to start with, but I want more plants next time. Grapes, maybe? Or berries? Olives, if we trade from the Bull Islanders. Who knows what we can make?"

"Only the Gods," Star said.

Autumn clasped her hand as well. "I have to greet the Tooth King and Gummy. Tell them how it went, and how we'll need to build some tents and cabins in the Flowering Fields, to keep people living there all season long."

"Don't take long," I said. "I've been away from you for long enough."

She laughed at that, gave my beard a pet, and headed over to the Tooth King. He had left his throne and stood next to her. They talked excited, Autumn motioning with her hands and describing what was needed to make the plants grow.

I looked at Star. A grim look on her face—the sadness that came from a dead friend.

"What is it?"

"Something at the back of my mind—a stray thought." She stared at the sky, a warm blue dotted with puffs of cloud. "The Tooth King got everything he wanted. White Hair argued over the Flowering Fields, but after she died, Muddy agreed. And the wounds she got—they were bad, but she could have survived. I've seen enough wounds to know. She could have lived to stop the Tooth King's plan."

What was she saying? "But White Hair died."

"She died—and Muddy gave the Tooth King the Fields, and now the Heap will have its plants." Her eyes fixed on the Tooth King. "I think—no, Red. I will not burden you with what I think. Another Wrong Death, along with so many, that gave us our plants and our fields of apples. More violence to help make us grow. If you knew my thoughts, it would only make you sad."

"Star—"

"Leave it." She waved to Autumn, who had finished her conversation. "Enjoy your time with the one you love."

Autumn returned from the Tooth King and rejoined us. "All done. I've made the plans. Now, my time is mine." She took my hands. "The Cook Cave, yes? Planting seeds until my arms ached has made me hungry. I've got a pouch full of teeth, straight from the Tooth King, and I want to buy enough meat, berries, and steamed roots to fill a mammoth, with plenty of fermented juice to wash it down." She glanced at Star. "You want to join us?"

"For a little," Star agreed. "Then I should find Spinner. See how she wants to spend the night."

"Does something worry you, Red?" Autumn took my hand.

What Star had mentioned—and the vision the Blood-Spiller had showed me. What would be the end of all that growing? Thin Noses would grow.

They'd outnumber the Broadheads then, and they already had better weapons. Their bows and throwing spears and finely-made axes. When it was all over, would the hills and mountains be empty?

I didn't know.

I held Autumn's hand tightly. "Nothing. Just how much I longed to be at your side."

"Oh, Red." She laughed a little and hugged me again. "You and your big heart."

We walked up the slope amongst music and falling flowers, and returned to the growing city of the Heap.

THE END

ABOUT OUR CREATORS

WRITER

MICHAEL PANUSH is a lifelong writer and Sacramento native. His books with Curiosity Quills include *The Stein* and *Candle Detective Agency, Volume 1: American Nightmares, Volume 2: Cold Wars*, and *Volume 3: Red Reunion*, all featuring a pair of occult detectives in the 1950s, Dinosaur Jazz, a story about a Lost World battling against the forces of modernization; *El Mosaico, Volume 1: Scarred Souls, Volume 2: The Road to Hellfire*, and *El Mosaico, Volume 3: Hellfire*, an occult Western about a Frankenstein bounty hunter. With Airship 27, he created *The Dagger Men, a Novel of the Clay Shamus*—a story of a golem detective. With Pro Se Press, he created *Ape's Honor*, a novel of Victoria's Ape, an alternate history adventure of a noble gentleman gorilla in a world of talking animals. His short fiction has been published in *Towers of Metropolis, George Chance: The Green Ghost, Pulp Mythology, Volume Two*, and *Bass Reeves, Frontier Marshal, Volume 5*.

His most recent work, *The Dead Sheriff, Volume 5: A Cold and Lonesome Grave* is out now from Airship 27.

He lives and teaches in Sacramento.

Follow him on the web at michaelpanush.com and on twitter at https://twitter.com/Michael_Panush

INTERIOR & COVER ILLUSTRATIONS

EARL GEIER - was born and raised in Chicago. He worked in the public library, at the Chicago Board of Trade, in a video store, and in a comic store. His favorite job was setting pins in a bowling alley. A self taught artist, he has done horror, fantasy and science fiction artwork in the role playing game industry for Fasa (Battletech, Mechwarrior, Shadowrun, Earthdawn), Chaosium (the H. P. Lovecraft based Call of Cthulhu and the Michael Moorcock based Elric), TSR (Dungeons and Dragons), Fantasy flight (DiskWars), Dark Conspiracy for GDW, Whispering Vault for Pariah Press, Robotech for Palladium, Unknown Armies (Atlas Games), West End Games and others.

He has illustrated books for Cemetery Dance, Chaosium, Gryphon and Subterranean Press, and covers for The Fandom Directory. In the comic book world he's had work published by Dark Horse Comics, Comiczone, Now, Innovation and DC Comics Paradox. His artwork was also featured as background in the series finale of the TV show Supernatural "Let it Bleed". And he likes to talk in the third person 'cuz it makes him feel important.

COVER COLORING ARTIST

ROB DAVIS - began his professional art career doing illustrations for role-playing games in the late 1980s. Not long after he began lettering and inking, then penciling comics for several small black and white comics publishers-most notably for Eternity Comics, which eventually became Malibu Comics in the 1990s, on their book SCIMIDAR with writer R.A. Jones. Branching out to other black and white publishers and eventually working at both DC and Marvel Rob worked on likeness-intensive comics like TV adaptations of QUANTUM LEAP and STAR TREK's many incarnations mostly on the DEEP SPACE NINE comics for Malibu. At Marvel, he worked on the Saturday morning cartoon adaptation of PIRATES OF DARK WATER. After the comics industry implosion in the late 1990's Rob picked up work on video games, advertising illustration, and T-shirt design as well as some small press comics like ROBYN OF SHERWOOD for Caliber. Rob continues to do the occasional self-published comic book as well as publisher and designer for his small-press production REDBUD STUDIO COMICS. Rob is Art Director, Designer, and Illustrator for the New Pulp production outfit AIRSHIP 27 partnered with writer/editor Ron Fortier. Rob is the recipient of the PULP FACTORY AWARD for "Best Interior Illustrations" in 2010 for his work on SHERLOCK HOLMES: CONSULTING DETECTIVE and has been nominated for the same award every year since. He works and lives in central Missouri with his wife, two children, and granddaughter.

THE CLAY SHAMUS

Sickle City is a magnet for the bizarre and unholy. When a legion of dead Roman soldiers converges on the modern metropolis, its salvation will lie in the hands of three unique warriors employed by Herman Holtz, a corrupt, bootlegging Jewish rabbi.

Emmet Clay is a golem built by Holtz' older brother, a powerful Russian rabbi. As Holtz' chief enforcer, he disguises himself as a detective. His two loyal allies are the beautiful and fiery Zipporah Sarfati, a deadly Sephardic swordswoman and the young Harvey Holtz, the rabbi's son; a devoted student of Jewish mysticism. Together the three of them must uncover the secret of the Dagger Men, a secret society of Jewish warriors that traces its origins back to the bloody destruction of Judea.

Writer Michael Panush (creator of El Mosaico and Stein & Candle series) offers up a terrific, fast-paced supernatural thriller filled with some of the most original, fanciful characters ever imagined. "The Dagger Men" is roller-coaster pulp ride that doesn't slow down until the very last page!

the DAGGER MEN
A Novel of the Clay Shamus

MICHAEL PANUSH

AN AIRSHIP 27 PRODUCTION

AIRSHIP27HANGAR.COM

NEW PULP

Pulp Fiction for a New Generation!

www.ingramcontent.com/pod-product-compliance
Lightning Source LLC
Chambersburg PA
CBHW070816250626
47170CB00006B/2120